THE

ARSONIST

By the same author

Mister Doggett
The Tidewaiter

Factual book

Thomas Doggett Coat & Badge
(300 years of history)

Suggested reading

The Coat by R.G. Crouch

Rob Cottrell started his genealogy business with his wife in 1996. Since then, he has indexed well over one hundred Thames & Medway riverside parishes, along with the apprenticeship binding records for the Company of Watermen & Lightermen of the River Thames.

This is his fourth book, which is not bad for someone who was diagnosed with Parkinson's in 2012.

He endeavours to prove there is life after Parkinson's.

This book is dedicated to a new generation
Ava Louise

The Eight Bells, Park Street, Hatfield

THE ARSONIST

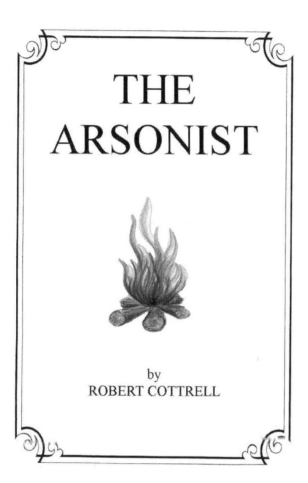

by
ROBERT COTTRELL

CHAPTER 1

Wedding & Funeral Bells

I, George Maynard, take thee, Sarah Harle, to be my lawfully wedded wife, to have and to hold, from this day forward, to love and to cherish, till death do us part, according to God's Holy Law. In the presence of God, I make this vow.

Sarah repeated her vows, and in less than ten minutes, on the sixth day of October 1833, George Maynard and Sarah Harle were pronounced man and wife at St. John the Evangelist Church in Lambeth, before a packed congregation. John Crawford and Lord David Gordon Hill sat at the back of the church, happy to witness their good friend marry his long-time sweetheart two months after winning the coveted Coat and Badge bequeathed by the famous actor and comedian, Thomas Doggett. Hill had officially retained the services of George Maynard, thereby protecting his young friend from the clutches of the Royal Navy.

Crawford and Hill apologised to the newly married couple for not being able to join them for their wedding breakfast at The Anchor on Southwark Bridge Road – the pressure of business always seemed to prevent them from enjoying the regular pleasures of life, which both men yearned for while others took for granted. Sir Richard Sharpe had already sent his apologies; he was in France, carrying out important repairs on his beloved farmhouse.

John Crawford had first met David Hill Esquire in the April of 1814, shortly after Napoleon, the emperor of France, had been forced to abdicate. Following the Treaty of Fontainebleau, Crawford was posted to France as a middle ranking diplomat within the Allied Joint Members of Staff, where David Hill became his aide. Throughout the years that followed, the two men remained good friends. Some even wondered if they were related.

In June of 1815, following Napoleon's escape from Elba and his subsequent one-hundred-day uprising, Crawford and Lord Hill hastily retreated from the French Capital to remain relatively close-by in the nearby province of Brussels.

After Waterloo, or, as the French preferred to call it, the Battle of Mont St. Jean, Crawford and Hill returned to Paris, where they remained until they were recalled to London nine years later. Subsequently, Crawford gained notoriety as a spy-master, and the newly appointed Lord Hill volunteered to remain by his side to act as his eyes and ears in the form of his enforcer.

After the wedding, Crawford and Hill returned to Whitehall by hackney carriage; they had been called to attend a private meeting with Earl Grey. The Prime Minister's reign had been a notable one; his greatest achievement was the overseeing of the passage of the reform bill concerning the House of Commons. He also successfully guided a bill to abolish slavery throughout the British Empire earlier that same year. As the years went by, Grey had become more conservative, thereby gaining a reputation for being overly cautious, especially when attempting to initiate additional far-reaching restructuring, particularly since he knew that the King was, at best, only a luke-warm supporter of his reforms.

Crawford had no idea why Grey had called the meeting, and Hill couldn't be bothered to ask – as he often liked to point out, he was simply the enforcer of Crawford's decisions.

As they entered Downing Street, both men were escorted into Grey's private office by one of his under-secretaries. Crawford judged the man to be about eighty if he was a day; he had a sullen expressionless face and looked extremely emaciated; his straight mouth with narrow set eyes seemed to give him a sinister facade; his attire, a shabby plain black suit which had seen better days, gave him the look of an undertaker. If Crawford had to choose a word to describe the man, *humourless* came to mind – the things that stick in your mind when you have played the spy for far too many years. Both men felt at ease once the under-secretary closed the office door behind them.

Grey was seated behind his old oak desk. The room was not overly decorated – plain and simple was the way Grey liked to operate and that was reflected in the way he liked his office. Viscount Melbourne, the Home Secretary, was seated on his right, and Edward Smith-Stanley, one of his Secretaries for War, was seated to his left. It appeared obvious to Crawford from their facial expressions alone that all three men had grave news to impart.

With a dismissive wave of his hand, Grey requested Crawford and Hill to take a seat. The Prime Minister seemed unsure about how to proceed with the agenda; he appeared nervous and fretful. He fumbled with the papers that were laid out before him on his desk, his fingers shook and the perspiration that was clearly visible on his brow gave him the look of an expectant father. He looked awkward about sharing his fears and insecurities with Crawford. Grey needed to ensure that whatever was on his mind came out right. He couldn't afford to be ambiguous. He knew his reputation was at stake – one wrong word or misunderstanding would prove fatal. He turned to his right and then to his left, looking for reassurance from cabinet fellows, but seeing none he glared directly into the face of John Crawford. But he remained silent; not a single word came from his mouth except the cursory good morning when the two men were ushered into Grey's domain. The Prime Minister drummed on the table with his right hand; this seemed to irritate Crawford. It was apparent that the Prime Minister was playing for time, or was he waiting for his cabinet colleagues to take up the reins? Hill looked smugly happy to witness a speechless politician – he had never seen one before.

Finally, Grey started to speak, only to be interrupted by Melbourne; the interruption was driven more by frustration than necessity. The Home Secretary's impatient demeanour overshadowed the Prime Minister's lack of confidence. Melbourne half-heartedly apologised for his untimely interruption by stating that the Prime Minister had many matters of state on his mind and asked their two guests to be patient. Crawford wondered if Melbourne's thin veil of feigned unity was true; after all, he could have given the Prime Minister more time to react, but the fact was that he hadn't.

Crawford had seldom been in Melbourne's company and speculated if the Home Secretary had been drawn to power; he seemed to act as if he would purposely step on anyone's toes to ensure he got his own way. Hill wasn't overly impressed by Melbourne either; upon reflection, he considered the man to have compulsions of gorging himself on the powerful recipe of supremacy and dominance, but one had to remember that Hill hated politicians more than he hated bankers and lawyers.

Crawford considered Melbourne to be lacking in any major achievements, achieving next to nothing in the way of grand principles during his time as Home Secretary; although, to be fair, he knew Melbourne to be genuine and honest – both being unusual qualities in politicians.

Crawford's original perception of Melbourne was wrong; he wasn't hungry for power or position – in fact, the opposite was true. He had used every available means under his disposal to shun prominence and power, although the rest of Crawford's rapid appraisal was most certainly accurate. Even Lord Hill considered Melbourne to be sincere and generous, which he thought to be highly uncharacteristic in a politician. Earl Grey slumped back into the fabric of his soft leather chair, leaving his Home Secretary to continue unabated. Melbourne spoke softly and with great compassion about the assassination of Spencer Percival, a crime against democracy that had occurred some twenty years earlier.

Percival was the Prime Minister when he had been assassinated within the lobby of the House of Commons by John Bellingham, a merchant who believed he had been unjustly imprisoned in Russia due to an alleged debt. Bellingham's principle grievance was against the elected government of the time who, in his mind, had done little to gain his release and repatriation to England.

Crawford and Hill knew the case reasonably well. Bellingham had pleaded insanity, but his plea had been discounted by the trial judge. John Bellingham was tried at the Old Bailey on Friday the fifteenth day of May 1812, where he stated that he would have preferred shooting the British Ambassador for his time spent in a Russian prison, insisting that, as a wronged man, he felt justified in killing the representative of his oppressors. Being found guilty of the crime, John Bellingham was hanged three days later at Newgate Prison.

Crawford bent forward and with his hand covering his mouth so as not to be heard he whispered to Lord Hill, 'why doesn't he mention the Cato Street conspiracy, surely that is more prevalent especially when a gang of revolutionaries conspired to murder the entire British cabinet along with the then Prime Minister Lord Liverpool'. Hill rubbed his chin as if to exaggerate thinking hard about the event, 'if I recall the episode, it was sheer luck that the conspiracy was uncovered by George Edwards, a police spy, who despite providing weapons and money to fund the plot. Today it might be classed as collusion.

Hill was getting bored, and, with his usual tact, enquired why both of these history lesson were so pertinent today, considering both Grey and Melbourne knew that George Edwards strings were being manipulated by none other than John Crawford who considered asking the same question but with more tact and diplomacy, but decided to let the matter go.

Melbourne disregarded Hill's sudden outburst and continued with his well-rehearsed sermon, asking if either man was aware that many similar assassination attempts had been foiled since Percival's time, but again failed to mention Cato Street. 'Both the Monarchy and the Parliament have grown profoundly concerned by the open hostility shown towards the Crown and Parliament, instigated by a misinformed rabble and foreign agents who worked tirelessly to destabilize the peace and stability of our great nation. The establishment is naturally concerned about their protection and safety, and they have requested us to establish a clandestine agency to protect them. The purpose of the agency or bureau – call it what you like – is to provide vital and pristine information while working undercover, and it is answerable only to the proper authorities.'

Crawford asked if a new agency was deemed necessary and why they couldn't recruit its membership from the ranks of the military or Peel's newly formed Metropolitan Police Force. Both the Prime Minister and the Home Secretary disagreed, 'In our considered opinion, the leader of the agency should be someone not connected with the military or the police, although we agree they could make up the junior ranks.'

It was Smith-Stanley's turn to speak; he pointed his thin index finger directly at Crawford and told him that, in his opinion, the only man he deemed capable of leading this new agency was none other than Mister Crawford. In the past, the police and the military have been found to be corrupt. 'We never know who to trust. Our country needs a man like you, Crawford', and with that the Prime Minister finally smiled.

Crawford knew he had been cornered; if he refused, he would be labelled a coward, but if he accepted, he had to agree to be answerable to politicians and the whims of the aristocracy. He knew the Crown had very little sway over the urges of politicians.

Smith-Stanley noticed Crawford's dilemma and tried to dangle a worm under the spy-master's nose. 'Parliament and the King would undoubtedly be most generous in light of your services. I have no doubt in due time they will consider doubling your salary, with the added possibility of a Lordship to boot.'

Crawford was getting visibly annoyed and started to fidget in his chair. 'The idea of a Lordship is abhorrent to me, the very notion of a title goes totally against my principles. If you think my only interest is to have a bloody title dangling in front of me, you certainly don't know me'. Smith-Stanley felt uneasy in his chair; he knew he had messed up and quickly tried to back-track by correcting his previous statement. 'Of course, any title would be conditional on your success, merit and ability, Mister Crawford. You'll only get recognition by merit and ability'.

'How many men do you think you need to man this agency?' Crawford asked. Melbourne quickly responded, 'The fewer the better. The chances of being infiltrated and discovered, especially by certain newspaper reporters, would be greatly reduced if the number was kept low. I suggest no more than ten, even six could get the agency started.'

Crawford still had mixed feelings about the idea; his greatest concern was what would happen if a Tory government should replace Grey's Whigs. 'Easy', replied Grey, 'we already have cross-party agreements at the highest levels, His Grace the Duke of Wellington and Sir Robert Peel have agreed with our proposals and have informed me that they have complete confidence in the formation of this secret service under your command. As for your other question regarding numbers, I agree with Melbourne that the number should be no more than ten at this time with the probability of at least one of your team based at Dover to watch over our borders and observe the arrivals and departures of known foreign agents'.

'Who will be responsible for selecting membership into the agency?' Crawford didn't want any political interference. Earl Grey turned to Melbourne and Smith-Stanley to ascertain if they were of one mind before giving his answer. 'The sole responsibility of getting the agency up and running will be yours, Mister Crawford; I assume you have no objection to Lord Hill being your deputy'.

'Would you be willing to put that in writing, Prime Minister?' Crawford responded, having a distinctly bad impression about the honesty of politicians due to his past experiences. Grey replied with a hint of annoyance in his voice, 'Will you not take the word of a gentleman, Mister Crawford?' To this, Crawford smiled before bluntly answering the Prime Minister's question – 'No'.

Grey had no choice and conceded surrender. Although he didn't want his name or signature to be associated with the agency, the Prime Minister was trapped. In order to achieve his objective, he had to sign away his right of remaining anonymous; nevertheless, he told Melbourne to countersign the order. Grey might have been outflanked, but he still thought that he had won this skirmish. The Prime

Minister shook Crawford's hand, and with that handshake, Grey had won his war.

On the carriage ride back to his lodgings at Westminster, Crawford thought about how dearly he would have loved to have Sir Richard Sharpe as a member of his team, but he knew Richard's best days were behind him. At a pinch, he knew Richard could handle himself, but a desk job deciphering paperwork was not his forte. The same could be said about Hill, but Crawford trusted Hill to cover his back, and that was more than adequate as a qualification for John Crawford, his only problem with Hill being managing his frequent outbursts.

In the days that followed, Crawford and Hill organised office space on one of the upper floors within Whitehall's west wing, where no one would be disturbed by frequent comings or goings. The occupants on the upper floors were well aware of Crawford's strange duties; even when recruits were being interviewed, it raised little suspicion. Twelve days after Crawford's meeting at Downing Street, he had the bases for his specialist team.

The first name on his list was Henry Trevaliant, the Englishman Sir Richard Sharpe had rescued from a French prison, a former debtor who spoke French fluently. Following the end of hostilities between England and France, Henry had established a tea importing business in Paris, but due to high inflation rates and with customers hard to find, he found himself unable to pay his bills and was consequently arrested and incarcerated within the debtors' prison. Henry was a highly intelligent man in his late thirties, smartly dressed and clean shaven. Next on the list was Richard Briggs – now in his early fifties, he had been a major in the 95th riffles, serving under Sharpe at Waterloo. Following the extended peace, Briggs had only been on half-pay for almost four years and, without the benefits of a pension, he was elated when Sharpe recommended his name to Crawford. Briggs idolised Sharpe and all he stood for, especially the way he had come up through the ranks – unlike Briggs, whose promotions came via his father's money. William Weaver was next on Crawford's list – a former prison officer who joined Peel's newly created Metropolitan Police Force. Weaver was acknowledged as a man of great courage who followed orders and never asked questions. Finally, after carefully pondering who the last person within the team should be, Crawford decided there was no reason why it shouldn't be a woman, preferably one of considerable beauty; he knew men always spoke freely to beautiful women. Crawford considered delegating the responsibility of choosing the last candidate to Hill, but on second thoughts he decided to make the choice himself.

Crawford consulted his private address book and considered three names from within its pages; however, as he flipped through the pages, he did not find the name he had at the back of his mind. He knew he had made a note of it somewhere – suddenly the name came back to him; it was his god-daughter, Lisabeth or Lizzie as he called her. As a young girl, she had a curious brain and loved solving puzzles. Whilst girls of her age were playing with dolls and learning home-craft, Lizzie enjoyed visiting museums and studying fossils and the wonders of creation; her favourite book at the time was entitled 'The Forces of Matter' –Lizzie was delighted when her parents purchased the book for fifteen shillings from Hatchards in Piccadilly. It didn't matter much to Lizzie that fifteen shillings only bought her a sixth edition reprint, although she would have preferred a signed first edition. She attended numerous lectures of Faraday's, but the story she found most amusing was one that the great man frequently imparted to his audience – Lizzie couldn't believe the story to be true, but Faraday assured his listeners that the tale was most accurate. His mentor Humphry Davy, the inventor of the miners lamp had repeatedly said that his greatest discovery was Faraday himself. Faraday's father had high hopes for his son, although self-taught and with a rudimentary education in reading, writing and mathematics, Davy recognised great potential in Faraday and took him under his wing, in 1831 Faraday discovered Electromagnetic Induction, thereby discovering that a varying magnetic field causes electricity to flow in an electric circuit.

Crawford had lost touch with Lizzie soon after being invited to her marriage; he and Hill had been posted back to France while Lizzie, her new husband, and her parents, Lord and Lady Sudbury, remained in England. Her father had been a wealthy timber merchant who held the monopoly of much of the pine, deal and spruce imported into London's Surrey Docks. With only those few clues to aid him, he assigned Hill to locate the woman he only knew as Lizzie Cotter. If ever they became reunited, Crawford made a promise to himself to renew their close family ties. It didn't take Hill too long to find her. Crawford's impatience got the better of him, and he arranged to meet Lizzie the following day at lunchtime inside the Red Lion Coffee House, just off Parliament Square. He hadn't told Hill or any other member of the newly created Government agency that Lizzie was like a second daughter to him – for now, that had to remain in the past and kept secret.

As soon as he entered the coffee house, he recognised Lizzie – she was still an attractive woman. Ten years ago, he had been a guest at her wedding, and in Crawford's eyes she hadn't aged. Sadly his duties in Europe had kept them apart, She was remained ever in his mind, Lizzie was now forty-three years old, but to Crawford, she looked no more than thirty. Dressed in a peacock blue carriage dress with gigot sleeves and a low waist-line that was suitably adorned with a sash tie, she looked amazing. The dress was ankle length and scantily trimmed. Her good looks weren't her only attributes; she was strong-willed and never allowed anyone to outsmart her. Lizzie's long flowing dark blonde hair, tied in an elegant bun exposing her slim neck thus creating an illusion that she was gliding into a room, swanlike, effortlessly gliding gracefully across the crystal glassy surface of a lake. Whenever she entered the room, everyone noticed. Crawford smiled to himself; Lizzie had grown into a beautiful woman. As well as being his god-daughter, Lizzie had unique talents that he intended to keep secret from his new team until they had assembled in their offices at Whitehall. Once he had briefed Lizzie regarding the job and the risks involved, nothing could hold her back; all her Christmases had come at once – she was overjoyed. Neither he nor Lizzie could inform anyone about the close family ties that their families enjoyed; both had to keep that matter under wraps, certainly for the time being.

On Monday, the sixteenth day of December, Crawford gathered his team for their first informal get-together at their new Whitehall offices. The offices had still not been decorated and as yet lacked desks, chairs and storage cabinets – everything that a secret agency needed, although perhaps the offices were so secret that no one had bothered to inform the decorators or removal men. The rooms were just basic shells, grubby and dirty, and in need of love and attention. The important thing for Crawford to consider was if he had got his social-mix just right. He kept the forenames of his team to himself; he purposely didn't want to give prior notice that one of the team members was a woman.

Crawford requested Hill to speedily beg, steal or borrow chairs and a table; he wanted the table to be of a certain design, but at this moment any table would suffice. The enforcer as usual did his job exceptionally well, and Crawford didn't ask where the items had come from.

Unbeknown to Crawford, Earl Grey had invited himself to this first gathering of the agency, he was accompanied by two of his closest advisors, Viscount Melbourne and Edward Smith-Stanley, all three remained towards the rear of the room and promised not to interfere.

Crawford introduced his team to each other after they were all comfortably seated. He started with David Hill, his second in command, followed by

Henry Trevaliant, Richard Briggs, William Weaver and finally Lizzie Drew. Lizzie arrived dressed in plain brown trousers with a matching great-coat that concealed her shapely body; her coat had a huge hood attached at the back to conceal her long flowing hair, but once she was introduced, she swiftly removed the hood to reveal her true identity – a woman. At first, there was a deadly silence which was followed by sheer disbelief, next came looks of confusion and shock, and finally horror and even embarrassment – what a cocktail of emotions! Even the Prime Minister looked shocked.

Crawford banged the table with his fist, calling for order, 'What you don't know, my friends, is that Lizzie has already been assigned an interesting task, and she has reported back to me with her deliverance just half an hour prior to this meeting. This young lady has already gone about her duties with great enthusiasm and gusto. Her reports will remain safe with me and not a word will be retold outside these four walls, but it just goes to show how stupid some gentlemen can be'.

Crawford used his voice and hand gestures to re-establish silence in the room. He had their attention and was about to embarrass members of his newly organised team. 'Gentlemen, I have no doubt that during the past week, each and every one of you have had the pleasure of being in Lizzie's company, but what is more importantly, especially for me, is that each and every one of you have confided a secret to her, a secret that, under normal circumstances you wouldn't want repeated. Well, in that case, you should have kept your secrets just that – secret'. Crawford continued with his oration, 'I can now reveal to you that one person sitting at this table today has a secret regarding his infidelity, one of you has a severe gambling addiction, one of you prefers to be in the company of young boys, and one of you recently entertained guests at a fashionable London restaurant and left without paying the bill'. Everyone glared at Lord Hill. 'Gentlemen, the point I am making is this: do you honestly think you would have disclosed any of this information to someone other than a beautiful young lady like Lizzie? I can assure each and every one of you that your inner most secrets are safe with me; I certainly will not hold any animosity against any of you. We all have our weaknesses'.

Everyone acknowledged Crawford's sound logic for appointing Lizzie as a member of the team and, without further ado, implicitly accepted Crawford's judgement, although all of them promised themselves to keep their thoughts securely locked inside their own heads in the future, or at least when in Lizzie's company. The tension in the room rapidly evaporated with half-hearted joviality breaking through to the surface. What the team didn't know was that Lizzie Drew had extraordinary talents – she was a cold-reader; she could read minds or convince her subjects that their minds were being read; some went further and called her a psychic, a term Lizzie always hotly disputed. She considered most psychics to be nothing more than charlatans, and although she knew people called her lots of things, she was not a charlatan; she simply used misdirection to develop skills of observation to create an illusion of having a sixth sense. Lizzie always maintained she couldn't read minds, but others thought she could, and that was all that mattered to John Crawford.

It was Hill's turn to spring a surprise by telling his fellow agency members that he too could read minds. 'My friends, it appears that one of our distinguished members of Parliament standing before us has, like all of us, a secret he would prefer us not to know about'. Hill studied the look of utter disdain on Crawford's face, not to mention the look of despair and shock on the faces of all three Parliamentarians. Hill immediately knew his prank had gone wrong and chose to back-track and keep quiet. Crawford knew his enforcer had difficulty in reading his own mind, let alone reading the minds of others. Hill's tomfoolery had totally misfired; the Parliamentarians remained aghast, but Lord David Gordon Hill, who considered himself to be a legend and enforcer, looked forlorn and stupid. On numerous occasions, he had thought that Hill went too far, and today's prank reinforced his view; what was the idiot thinking!

Crawford quickly defused his embarrassment by suggesting that the group remain inside the room, while he spoke privately to Earl Grey, Viscount Melbourne and Edward Smith-Stanley in the adjacent corridor. As Crawford passed by Hill to leave the room, he whispered 'prick' to his friend, who silently whispered back, 'What?'. Hill just didn't get it!

Everyone wanted to talk with Lizzie Drew; they wanted to find out everything about her – what she did when she wasn't reading minds, where she lived, was she married? – but Lizzie remained tight-lipped, giving nothing away. Eventually, the team started chatting about the agency and the roles they thought each should progress on. All of them, including Lizzie, considered themselves well-matched for field work. Crawford had already appointed Samuel Vickers as clerk to keep notes and records; he had enough brains to sort out any incoming intelligence and break simple codes. Vickers would be required to report back to Crawford. Samuel relished the opportunity to excel behind a desk, by solving quandaries – he wasn't up to being a fighting operative.

When Crawford returned to the office, he agreed with the choices each member of his team had made for themselves. 'I haven't a shred of hesitation in declaring that given your natural talents you have all made the right choice. It may surprise you to know that I picked each and every one of you for a specific reason – you are all unattached, widows, widowers or bachelors, none of you have dependants to support or worry about. From now on these are your new family; bond as such and watch out for each other and, most importantly, protect each other as a family'.

Crawford spoke separately to Lizzie, informing her why he was happy that she would be out in the field. 'This is based on fact', he told her, 'simple-minded idiots love to brag about their exploits, and I have no doubt you will be a good listener. But be careful, some of the idiots you'll listen to will have evil intentions, so I say it once again, *be careful*'.

Crawford moved over to speak to Trevaliant, 'You have sampled prison life and all it has or doesn't have to offer. I am more than certain that you'll be able to keep yourself safe by remaining in the background, keeping yourself out of trouble to eavesdrop on confidential confessions, plots or conspiracies'. Crawford continued with his appraisal of Henry Trevaliant. 'You speak fluent French as well as German. And English, of course; you'll be a great asset to me and the team. Eventually, you'll be posted to Dover, where you will be my ears and eyes and track any undesirables wishing to enter or exit England'.

Richard Briggs waited eagerly to hear what the spy-master thought about him, but instead he by-passed Briggs to talk to Weaver. 'William, I have spoken to Sir Robert Peel about you, he tells me you're one of his brightest officers, but since I am not Sir Robert Peel, I alone will judge if you can live up to my standards – though I do have great confidence in your abilities'.

Crawford came back to look at Richard Briggs. 'My good friend Sir Richard Sharpe was at Waterloo, where he was with the Duke throughout the peninsular campaign, and he informs me that you can be foolish at times. Besides being head-strong, compulsive and inclined to disobey orders, you are also a gambler and a womaniser. I think you and Lord Hill will get along just fine. Maybe the two of you will become great friends, as you certainly share many attributes'.

Richard Briggs appeared embarrassed, while Lord Hill grinned and winked at him.

Crawford went on to update his team about his discussion with Grey. 'It appears, my friends, that our team should remain elusive, as we don't officially exit. If we break any laws of another country, we'll be on our own. England will not protect or recognise us and will not offer us aid. If we should die whilst performing our duties, our loved ones will not be officially recompensed – do you all understand?'

'Now you are all fully aware of the pitfalls and dangers we face. If any of you wants to withdraw, now is the time to let me know. I will fully understand and respect your decisions – please raise your hand now'.

To Crawford's utter surprise, the only hand raised was Hill's. Crawford knew his friend could be an obstinate bugger, but he hadn't considered he would ever contemplate leaving his side.

Crawford smiled when he realised Hill merely wanted to make a point, albeit a point that was important to him. He wanted Crawford's remarks about the dangers to be recorded within the minutes. Crawford laughed at his old friend – 'As we don't officially exist, there will be no minute taking, now or in the future'.

'Them buggers in Downing Street, Whitehall and Horse Guards will always cover their fat arses, but when they realise we are their only line of defence – or attack, for that matter – it will be us who will deal with the murderers, assassins and revolutionaries – and you can guarantee that most of our adversaries will be either totally crazy or insane. Our so-called superiors must understand that without people like us, they will never be able to truly sleep soundly in their beds'.

There were only two vocations within English society that Hill loathed more than politicians – bankers and lawyers. He was whole-heartedly against both professions because, in his mind, they had both plotted against him by telling him that he was nothing more than a paid servant; however, if that were true, he told all of them they weren't paying him enough.

Crawford could only guess why David's hatred of bankers, politicians and lawyers ran so deep, but he assumed it had something to do with him being forced to sell most of the land from his newly acquired estate following the death of his father. Hill may have inherited a title, but in doing so, he had also inherited every debt that his father had accumulated.

Hill turned to look at his good friend, who was speaking to him. 'Instead of the King expressing feelings of deep regret over our graves and ring our funeral bells, I would dearly love to live long enough to ring their bloody bells'. Crawford reminded his friend, 'Be careful what you wish for'.

With that comment still ringing in Hill's ears, he left the room mimicking the sound of bells – clang, clang, ding, dong, clang – followed by one of his favourite sayings – 'For whom the bell tolls'.

Crawford thought it all too funny for words and was pleased when Hill's sour mood had lifted; the bugger was actually laughing and singing.

Oranges and lemons,
Say the bells of St. Clement's.
You owe me five farthings,
Say the bells of St. Martin's.
When will you pay me?
Say the bells at Old Bailey.
When I grow rich,
Say the bells of Shoreditch.
When will that be?
Say the bells of Stepney.
I do not know,
says the great bell at Bow.

Hill popped his head around the open door of the office and sang at the top of his voice –

Here comes a candle to light you to bed,
And here comes a chopper to chop off your head.

Chop, chop, chip, chop, the last man is dead.

Hill's voice gradually faded as he strolled happily along the corridor towards the stairs and into the outside world.

'When will you pay me, say the bells of Old Bailey?'

CHAPTER 2

Resignation

Earl Grey invited Crawford back to Downing Street the following week. The message simply said 'Please come at your earliest convenience, and please come alone'. Upon meeting the Prime Minister, Crawford noticed how he had changed in the past week, his red puffy eyes indicated he had not been sleeping too well. He appeared restless and agitated, and it was if he was struggling to cope. Crawford thought this meeting was not going to be overly cheerful. Eventually, Grey confided in his spy-master, 'I have received this strange coded note, it was left for me in the lobby of the House of Commons'. Crawford examined the single dirty, mud-stained sheet of paper to ascertain whether it had any watermark or any other indication that would point to the identity of the writer or to see whether the message offered any clue about the same. Sadly, he found nothing. The code was written in French, and although he spoke the language, the wording remained obscure to him even after reading it over and over again. Promising to report back within a few days, he thanked Grey for his time and ordered a hackney to take him back to Whitehall.

Crawford was still clutching the piece of paper in his hand as he entered his private office on the upper floor of Whitehall, where Henry Trevaliant and Sam Vickers were busy working on a tricky test code set for them by Lizzie Drew. Crawford placed the message in the centre of their desk and requested the two men to 'hold everything you're doing and tell me what you make of this', pointing to the grubby message.

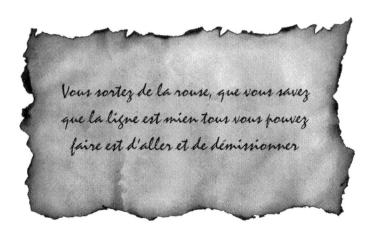

'I can see it's written in French but what does it say, Trevaliant? You're the expert.' Henry Trevaliant studied the grubby sheet of paper and translated the contents for the benefit of the others:

'To take you of out of the rouse, you know the line is mine, all you can do is go and resign'.

Trevaliant considered the message very poetic, possibly the work of a female, 'but that's just a guess'.

John Crawford hadn't thought about the sex of the composer, but he was happy that Trevaliant had translated the message exactly as he had. However, neither man was any closer in deciphering the meaning of the code. 'Now that we're all aware of the contents of the message, I suggest we get down to work out its hidden meaning. All I can tell you at this stage is that the note was left for the Prime Minister inside the lobby of Parliament this morning. I suggest we split the note into its three separate components. In this way, the message might reveal its true meaning quicker than if we try to unravel the whole code in one go'. That made perfect sense to everyone in the room.

Briggs studied the final line of the code. 'It seems evident the writer wants Grey to resign as Prime Minister, that much is clear, but why?' Weaver gazed closer at the second line. 'What line is the writer referring to?'

Lizzie wandered over to the desk to take a closer look at the message and whispered to herself, 'To take you out of the rouse'. She repeated the line again and again until it burnt into her mind. Suddenly, Lizzie laughed and gently slapped Weaver's rosy red cheeks. 'We're such stupid buggers! Read the line again, this time literally – take the 'u' out of the word rouse, and what are you left with?'

William took a step back as if he had been asked a trick question. Realising that this was not the case, he turned and looked at Lizzie to reveal his answer – 'Rose, of course'. Weaver exclaimed, 'But it's spelt wrong'.

'Don't worry about that, John. So now we have the word "rose", which leads us nicely to the next line of the code, and more specifically to the word "line". The code tells us the line is not his'. Weaver remained puzzled when he gently put the two words together – 'rose-line'. 'What is a rose-line?' he enquired.

Lizzie told him the answer as Crawford and his team stood back to admire the woman's logic and knowledge. 'The Rose Line is a fictional name given to the Paris meridian and to the sunlight line defining the exact time of Easter. So, besides the prestige of having such an important line run through your country, it also has religious connections'.

'Bloody hell, that's all we need', replied Hill, 'a bloody religious fanatic, they're the worst types of lunatics'.

'I assume the code is written in French for a good reason,' Sam said. 'The French have constantly argued that the meridian line, or the zero degree longitude should be in Paris, whilst here we English maintain the line should run through Greenwich. If Bonaparte had beaten us at Waterloo, the French would have gotten their way and moved the meridian line into the heart of the French capital'.

Richard Briggs sympathised somewhat with the French argument, explaining to Vickers, 'Paris is the capital of France whereas Greenwich is just a small village in Kent to the south-east of London. In historical times, the suffix "-wich" simply meant a dwelling place; in Anglo-Saxon times, Greenwich translated simply to a "green dwelling place", hardly a renowned location for such a significant phenomenon as the east meeting the west'.

Vickers, sensing an argument brewing, responded by explaining to Briggs, 'Are you aware that it was John Flamsteed who calculated the formula for converting solar time into mean time? And it was Flamsteed who published his set of conversation tables sixty years ago to support and prove his claims. Two years after submitting his tables, he was appointed the first Astronomer Royal and moved to the new Royal Observatory at Greenwich. You understand me, Richard? I said Greenwich, not fucking Paris'.

Crawford, like the rest of team was getting frustrated and annoyed by the heated argument between Briggs and Vickers. He shouted at both men to stop behaving like children. 'I assume that neither of you are aware of what came next? Well, Flamsteed had a young assistant named Edmund Halley. It was he who misappropriated much of Flamsteed's work and passed it on to Isaac Newton. It was John Flamsteed who accurately calculated the solar eclipses as well as the earliest known sightings of the plant Uranus, although he originally mistook the planet for a distant star'. From the stark expressions on the faces of both Briggs and Vickers, it was clear that neither man knew what Crawford was talking about. For the sake of peace and quiet and to bring the argument to a speedy conclusion; Crawford decided to enlighten both of them. 'All of what I have told you is correct, but for the life of me I never understood why Halley had the comet named after him when it was Flamsteed who calculated its orbit, and why Newton was honoured with a knighthood. To suggest that the relationship between the three men was anything but strained is very much an understatement. John Flamsteed was ordained as a church deacon in 1675, which must have curtailed his innermost thoughts towards Halley and Newton, and I suggest from now on you both keep your thoughts to yourselves'.

'Gentlemen, let's get back to reality. Why would the French kick up such a fuss about the positioning of the meridian line now? It doesn't make sense, let alone the suggestion that a British Prime Minister should resign over the issue. This is beyond me, it's completely illogical. Nevertheless, I will return to Downing Street this afternoon to relate our findings'.

Crawford was welcomed back to Downing Street just after three o'clock by Viscount Melbourne who ushered Crawford into a small private room towards the rear of the building. The room was sparsely decorated and inadequately adorned by three chairs and a small table; the closed plain brown curtains acted as a blackout, so much so that two candles were strategically placed neatly upon the table. Even so, to Crawford the room looked like a place of interrogation rather than a place to have a cosy chat in.

Once the two men were alone, Crawford explained his teams meaning of the code, although, he was unsure why Earl Grey had been the receiver of such a note, unless Melbourne was conscious of any diplomatic rift between France and England.

Melbourne thought for a second before replying. 'None what so ever Mister Crawford, but I have been requested by the Prime Minister to give you this, which I found on the cabinet room table before lunch'. Crawford instinctively knew it was another message, as the first message had been so easily deciphered. Melbourne feared that the second message had unnerved the Prime Minister, and he considered Earl Grey to be on the very brink of resignation. Crawford quickly glanced at the note, noticing it was much like the first – written on grubby dirty paper and, again, written in French. Crawford stuffed the note unceremoniously into his waistcoat pocket, thanked Melbourne for his time and left the residence of the Prime Minister and returned to his waiting hackney carriage to return to the relative comfort of his own office at Whitehall.

Upon his return to Whitehall, only Samuel Vickers was at his desk. The others were taking a late lunch, discussing their earlier success in solving the crazy code. 'Sam', Crawford shouted, 'get the team together. We have another code to work on, but this time I fear it will take much longer to unravel. Tell the team I will accept no excuses for non-attendance other than news of their unforeseen deaths'. Samuel knew where the team had gone and by five o'clock everyone where arrayed inside the office, ready for Crawford's briefing. 'The reason for getting you all together in the office is that I didn't want to repeat myself. I also want to hear your theories about how these messages seem to be accelerating. I need your opinions: are we dealing with a joker or a madman, a revolutionary or a lunatic, or a religious fanatic?

Whatever you think the answer might be, I need to have your opinions, and quickly'.

Crawford laid the dirt-stained note on the desk, and his team gathered around him as he solemnly enquired, 'What do you make of this?'

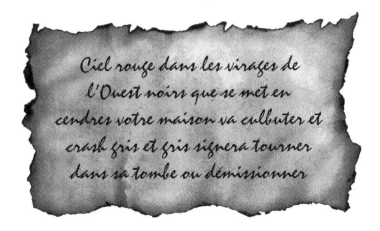

Ciel rouge dans les virages de l'Ouest noirs que se met en cendres votre maison va culbuter et crash gris et gris signera tourner dans sa tombe ou démissionner

Lizzie suggested it would be advisable 'if Trevaliant could translate it for us before progressing to what we make of it'.

Crawford apologised, as Trevaliant translated the code into English.

'Red sky in the west turns black as ash; your house will tumble and crash. Grey will turn and grey will sign, turn in his grave or forced to resign'.

'Very poetic', Lizzie sarcastically pointed out; 'I would stake my reputation on the fact that this code is definitely the work of a woman', while the rest of the team looked on completely perplexed, pondering about the significance of the message – was it a threat or a warning? Sam Vickers spoke first, '*Grey will turn and grey will sign* seems clear enough, but *turn in his grave or resign* seems ominous to me'. Both Vickers and Weaver nodded their heads in agreement before joining the conversation, 'But the line about the red sky in the west turning black as ash certainly points to an arson attack, but whose house will tumble and crash? I assume there's nothing more?'

Everyone put forward various theories, but they were only theories, and their biggest problem was that there was no clue to reveal where and when the event would take place. Trevaliant even quoted a passage from the Bible attributed to Jesus: '*red sky at night, shepherd's delight*, but surely this would indicate good news, basically meaning good weather will follow'. Lizzie commented on the 'black as ash' line, 'Could this symbolise charcoal?' she asked. Crawford thought about Lizzie's remark and agreed that the representations of fire were certainly present. 'We're still left with the quandary regarding whose house will tumble and crash'. They had to consider if the message was sincere or not, or was it solely meant to create fear and panic? –if the latter was true, the writer of the note had certainly succeeded in his objectives.

The meeting was adjourned well after midnight without any concrete progress having been made. Everyone was tired. A new dawn would brighten the eastern sky on Tuesday the second day of July 1834.

Crawford and Hill returned to Downing Street on the tenth of July for another meeting with the Prime Minister. They were greeted at the front door of number ten by Viscount Melbourne, who looked visibly shaken. It was Crawford and Hill who had intended to give Grey negative news, but it was soon apparently that Melbourne's news was significant. 'Come in gentlemen,' Melbourne guided his guests to the cabinet room where the Duke, Robert Peel and Smith-Stanley were waiting patiently for their arrival. Melbourne sprawled in his chair as Crawford and Hill waited with bated breath to hear about the calamity that had overtaken Downing Street.

'Mister Crawford, I fear I have some sad news to impart. Earl Grey resigned yesterday. He had had enough. He's left the country in my hands until an election or an agreement can be reached with my fellow parliamentarians. In a manner akin to the Roman prefect Pontius Pilate, he has washed his hands of the country's affairs and walked away. Last night, he left with his wife, Mary Elizabeth Ponsonby, and their family for their home in Howick, Northumberland, to *forever leave behind the murky world of politics* – his words, not mine'. Hill smiled at such a confession, it was music to his ears.

Hill wondered if the house referred to in the riddle was Downing Street or if it could possibly be Howick or any of the other retreats of the Prime Minister. Everyone guessed, but they were all pissing into the wind. Wellington asked Crawford, 'Have you any news on the message Melbourne gave you?' Crawford seemed to be downcast and replied, 'Best not to give you more bad news today'. Peel reluctantly replied, 'I'll take that as a no then!'

Days went by, and the days turned into weeks, and the weeks turned into months without anything of note occurring. Crawford wondered if the message had become invalid now that Grey had departed from office. It was not until three months had gone by, on the sixteenth of October, that reality hit everyone hard. The house referred to in the coded message was the mother of democracy – both houses of Parliament, the Lords' and the Commons', and the Palace of Westminster. It suddenly became obvious to Crawford that the red sky in the west represented Westminster, and red signified a fire. No one had imagined an arson attack of this magnitude in the very heart of London. Crawford recalled witness statements regarding the great fire of 1666 when onlookers described the utter devastation to the court of enquiry that when St. Paul's burned, molten lead from the roof ran in the street making the pavements too hot to walk on. Crawford felt sick in the pit of his stomach as he pictured the scene of absolute destruction. Last night the very heart of democracy had all but been obliterated from the city's skyline. Both Houses of Parliament were destroyed along with most of the other buildings on the site. Westminster Hall was saved largely due to heroic fire-fighting efforts of the newly established London Fire Brigade, and a change in the direction of the wind during the night. A strong south-westerly breeze had fanned the flames along the wood-paneled and narrow corridors into St Stephen's Chapel. Shortly after Braidwood's Fire Brigade's arrival, totaling twelve engines and sixty-four firemen, the roof of the chapel collapsed, the resultant noise was so loud that the watching crowds thought there had been another Gunpowder plot explosion.

Sadly the newly formed river brigade proved ineffectual due to the tide being so low and left the scene without rendering any worthwhile assistance.

The only other parts of the Palace to survive were the Jewel Tower, the Undercroft Chapel, the Cloisters and Chapter House of St Stephen's and Westminster Hall. Surprisingly, no one bothered to ask if there were any fatalities; the politicians were more worried that their precious bricks and mortar had in part been destroyed.

From their office at Whitehall, the agency knew they were dealing with a fanatic, but they didn't know if the culprit was of the religious type or just enjoyed starting fires. Hill asked Crawford, 'Why didn't we ask our friendly barmaids or our many watermen associates if any rumours were bubbling away in discontented minds. We know from experience that gossip flies up and down this river like fledglings departing the nest. Every fanatic and lunatic loves to boast about their exploits, they crave recognition and fame; they have to tell someone about their evil deeds, otherwise there is no point in committing the crime. And what is better than confiding in barmaids with big tits; it serves to arouse them'. Crawford was dumfounded, not by Hill's tone, but by his own inaction. Why hadn't he even considered talking to the barmaids prior to the attack on Parliament, and what is more, why hadn't he even considered the Houses of Parliament to be a target?

Crawford gazed across the table at Hill and asked, 'Who would you like to interview first, the watermen or the buxom barmaids?' Hill chuckled, 'Who do you think, John'? Crawford decided not to answer Hill's remark. His womanising was well known among his fellows.

The morning after the fire, the Royal Family verified that they had witnessed the blaze from as far away as Windsor. Only Melbourne, Wellington, Peel and a small group of politicians knew of the existence of the coded messages, and they had to keep it that way. It was left to Melbourne as the newly appointed Prime Minister to issue a statement affirming the fire had been caused by accidently burning excessive amounts of old papers and tally-sticks deep within the bowels of the Parliament. Crawford recommended that Melbourne should include the following within his statement – 'The nation is most grateful to Superintendent James Braidwood and his fellow firemen from the London Fire Establishment for their bravery in quickly bringing the blaze under control without loss of life'. Crawford knew from experience that the chaos and panic outside Parliament must have greatly hindered the fire crew in their arduous task.

It was all a lie, of course. Except the bit about James Braidwood and his men – they had indeed exhibited commendable bravery.

Rumours, originating from the lips of barmaids, were circulating within the city, pointing to a small group of Irish travellers who had threatened revolution within the city. Similar gossip had spread among the river folk, but Crawford considered it all to be bogus, a red herring to put the authorities off the scent of the real villain. It was like the chicken and the egg syndrome: what came first? No doubt one had heard the gossip and passed it on like Chinese Whispers. Crawford had to quickly put an end to these ridiculous tittle-tattle or, to be more accurate, he had to get the Prime Minister to issue a further statement to put an end to all this tittle-tattle. If they didn't, every Irishman in London would be persecuted as a fire raiser.

On Monday, the twentieth day of October 1834, acting on the instructions from John Crawford, another statement was hurriedly prepared for the Prime Minister to read out to the press. He confirmed that the tragic fire was nothing more than an accident, and not the result of a deliberate attack by a person or persons unknown. Melbourne even brought forward numerous highly respectable witnesses to confirm his statement. Lord Hill afterwards remarked, 'politicians find it very easy to lie! Crawford turned away in disgust; he wasn't going to be drawn into an argument with Hill even though he knew his remark to be true.

London was swiftly brought back from the brink of anarchy and chaos. There had been some rioting and looting due to unfounded speculation concerning an Irish connection; however, this had been snuffed out thanks to the quick thinking of Crawford. Since he was from Scotland, he knew what it was like to be persecuted for not being English. His secret service agency had only been in existence for less than a year, but they seemed powerless to alter the mood of a nation that was already depressingly subdued. The fire at Westminster had everyone on edge: if fires could be started inside Parliament – then no place was safe.

Matters only got worse in November when Melbourne was brushed aside by Wellington, who quickly formed his government. However, after a mere twenty-seven days in power, he was replaced by Sir Robert Peel.

Life spans in politics were getting shorter, and not so sweet. Not that Lord David Hill was bothered – he hated politicians, lawyers and bankers.

The agency was still left with the task of finding a madman. Questions were being asked by politicians of various persuasions; it isn't an easy task to juggle balls in the air whilst their pay masters changed every five minutes. 'Who are we answerable to now'? Hill enquired after Crawford. 'I'm sure you're just as confused as me, David' – which was true.

It isn't an easy task to juggle balls

Earl Grey
Resigned 9th July 1834

Viscount Melbourne
16th July-14th November 1834

His Grace the Duke of Wellington
14th November-10th December 1834

Sir Robert Peel
10th December 1834-8th April 1835

1834
The year of four Prime Ministers

CHAPTER 3

Conspiracies!

If 1834 was a year for political musical-chairs, Crawford wondered what the new year had in store. He didn't have to wait too long for an answer. The Prime Minister requested his and Hill's presence to attend a covert meeting with members of his staff at Downing Street. The meeting had been arranged for ten in the morning on Wednesday the seventh of January. Crawford and Hill were in need of exercise and fresh air and decided to walk the short distance from their office at Whitehall to Downing Street. Due to the stink from the Thames, fresh air had of late become a precious commodity. Thankfully, the weather was dry, with a light breeze blowing from the north. Upon their arrival at Downing Street, the two men were met by three of Sir Robert Peel's new diplomatic police team, who barred their entry. Crawford produced his identity papers to indicate that he was himself a head of a government department, but to his utter astonishment Crawford and Hill were unceremoniously told that the Prime Minister was not to be disturbed today. Crawford checked his watch; it was already ten minutes past ten and Crawford hated being late. 'Just knock on the door, I'm sure the Prime Minister has forgotten our meeting and will vouch for us'. Sadly, Crawford's pleas went unanswered.

To begin with, the security officers seemed apologetic, but after fifteen minutes of arguing on the doorstep of number ten, the impasse was attracting the unwanted attention of onlookers from the direction of the intersection with Whitehall. The police officers were getting nervous and fidgety. Crawford kept checking his watch – he was nearly twenty minutes late for his appointment with Sir Robert Peel and was getting anxious whilst Hill was beginning to enjoy himself, sensing a fight coming, brewing.

'There's only one way we're getting inside today', Hill explained to Crawford, 'and that's by sheer force, whether you like it or not. I think your way of dealing with this has proved ineffectual, but I'm more than happy to display my own brand of diplomacy'. Hill glanced at Crawford for approval, but there was no obvious authorisation seemed to come. Then Crawford replied in a soft voice, 'No, do what you have to do'.

Hill had grounded two of the officers before the door to number ten opened, revealing an open-mouthed, frightened footman who stood in front. Two excited female servants and a horrified Sir Robert Peel were standing no more than two yards further back. Peel was just in time to witness the final officer go crashing to the pavement, courtesy of a right upper-cut delivered by a cheerful Lord Hill. 'I might be double their age, but it takes more than three buffoons to stop me in my tracks'. Hill casually stepped over the prostrated officers, careful not to add to their injuries, and strolled inside the passage of the Prime Minister's residence, with Crawford suitably embarrassed by the incident following in his wake.

Crawford, noticing that the footman had an injured leg and walked with a cane, offered to close the door behind him.

Crawford apologised for Hill's hostility and immediately extended his right hand for Peel to shake. Sir Robert appeared confused and, without thinking, offered his own hand, but Crawford couldn't help thinking that all the unpleasantness could have been avoided if Sir Robert hadn't told his security officers to keep everybody out. Needless to say, Hill hadn't bothered to offer any apology or hand shake; his detest of officialdom had preceded him. Peel ushered his guests into the parlour where his political friends were already seated, introducing his two guests as members of the newly formed protection agency. 'This is Mister Crawford, gentlemen, and his associate Lord Hill. Please accept my apologies, gentlemen. I completely forgot about our appointment'. Hill turned to Crawford and thought to himself, 'All this violence could have been avoided if only we had a Prime Minister who could remember things'. Crawford, however, didn't rise to Hill's bait, but Hill wasn't going to let the matter rest – he raised his eyebrows as if to say 'You can't expect anything else from a Tory'.

Crawford was feeling self-conscious about his untidy appearance. There were specks of blood on his shirt and jacket; he involuntarily struggled to straighten his thinning grey hair and wispy beard but found his endeavours useless. 'I really should have got my hair and beard trimmed before today', he thought to himself. He hadn't been listening when Peel asked him if he needed a clean shirt or wanted his footman to wipe the stains from his jacket. Crawford looked embarrassed as he stood motionless in the doorway leading from the passageway into the parlour room. He fidgeted and felt his cheeks burn and glow as he came abruptly out of his daydream when Hill softly whispered, 'Come into my parlour, said the spider to the fly'.

As both men entered the parlour room, the Prime Minister introduced his guests to his ministers, or his 'inner circle', as he preferred to call them. It was Hill's turn to look out of place; he hated listening to politicians and couldn't bear to be in the same room as them, but he bit his tongue for the sake of his friend. Crawford retained his embarrassment as he sat down in the nearest chair, leaving Hill to stand by his side. Henry Goulburn, Peel's home secretary, looked amused at Hill's predicament; however, the smile was speedily wiped from Goulburn's face when Hill, somewhat forcibly, sat so close to the home secretary that it caused the man to vacate his chair – he had, not so gently, dug him in the ribs. Peel looked horrified, but Crawford, although dismayed, calmed the situation by changing the subject. 'What did you want to talk to me about, Sir Robert?' Crawford was at last back in control of himself.

Peel's off-handed disposition hadn't changed. Even though he respected Crawford, he liked the way he went about his job, and most importantly, he liked the way he got the job done. 'We've received another coded message', he replied. Crawford asked to see the note. He read it carefully. It was again written in French, and he had no doubt that Peel already knew the contents of the message. Crawford asked if he could take the message back to his Whitehall office where his team could dissect and test the code for any hidden clues. Not that he expected to find any – he just wanted to get Hill out of Downing Street to the relative safety of the agency's base.

The two men walked in silence back to Whitehall, neither taking the trouble to look at the other. When they arrived at Whitehall, Crawford was furious and demanded an explanation for assistant's his rudeness, asking if it was really necessary to make life so uncomfortable for Goulburn by forcing him to give up his seat. 'You're so vindictive David. What's the matter with you? Do you find it so hard to behave in civilised society? You may well have ruined our chances to establish this agency under our rules. It seems that if you cannot act in a proper fashion, then our paymasters will inflict arduous rules upon us – is that what you want?' Hill was speechless and shrugged his shoulders, wondering what all the fuss was about. 'Don't know why the bugger was there,' he replied, 'the pip-squeak didn't utter one single word throughout the entire meeting'.

Henry Trevaliant and William Weaver had often seen their superiors arguing, but seldom like this. Crawford's reddening face looked ready to explode, and to make matters worse, Hill couldn't maintain his stern-faced composure any longer – he burst into laughter, finding the morning highly amusing.

'I bloody give up on you David, why do you constantly behave the way you do?' Crawford sternly asked. 'We set the buggers right though, didn't we,

John?' Hill was talking as if the incident was nothing more than a playground brawl instead of a skirmish inside the Prime Minister's London home.

Crawford glared at Hill, 'we didn't put any bugger right, David, but I fear you most certainly did'. Hill was getting thoroughly bored with the bickering and asked his friend if he wanted tea or whisky. Crawford stared angrily at Hill in utter disgust, wondering what to do with the man; he removed the crumbled grubby note from his jacket pocket and handed it to Trevaliant for a translation before excusing himself to clean up and replace his stained shirt. Trevaliant read the note and passed it across to Weaver. Assuming the code was written in French, he simply passed it back to Crawford on his return.

Crawford ordered Willie to locate every member of the agency. 'Get them back here; this message seems just as sinister as the first, and, I fear, much harder to understand'. William informed him that Henry Trevaliant must be half way to Dover by now, but the look on Crawford's face told William that that was of no consequence, and he would have to get Briggs back to London as soon as possible. Hill turned to look at John Crawford. 'None of us solved the coded message regarding the fires at the Houses of Parliament'. Crawford was painfully aware of their failings, but he wished Hill didn't have to keep reminding him.

By six o'clock, the entire team was back at Whitehall, with six pairs of weary eyes looking down at the grubby torn sheet of stained paper. Trevaliant placed the torn sheet of paper alongside the earlier message before he translated it into English.

Pas le dernier incendie de Londres,

il y aura plus.

Où il finira ?

Dans le domaine des chapeaux.

'*Not the last fire for London, there will be more. Where will it end? In the field of hats.*'

Lizzie was the first to speak. 'The writer makes it clear that he or she intends to start at least one more fire'. But pointing towards the line 'there will be more', she hesitated. 'Have you noticed anything different about this message?' Her colleagues obviously hadn't noticed anything except another threat. What was Lizzie thinking? 'It's not poetic this time. I think… although the note is written on identical paper, we have two arsonists provoking us'.

'You could be right in your assumptions, Lizzie', Crawford agreed. 'I *know* I am', she retorted.

Briggs ambled towards the desk; he had been listening intently and thumbed the last line of the message. '*in the field of hats* – an interesting choice of words, I've checked various maps of London and the surrounding counties; there's no obvious reference to a field of hats. I considered St. Martin's in the Fields, but fear it has little association with a field of hats'. William wondered about the line 'where will it all end' and considered if there might be a hidden meaning such as the end of the year, but they were all guessing. Like with the previous code, this time too it simply made no sense even to Lizzie's inquisitive mind.

Crawford suggested that, except William, the whole team should get a good night's sleep. 'We have plenty of street-walking to do tomorrow. Mister Weaver here', pointing to William, 'will check the maps for any observable connections to a field of hats'.

'Before we retire for the night, sir', Lizzie was most anxious to get her proposal heard, 'wouldn't it be favourable if we split ourselves into smaller groups, whereby any lead could be brought back to William to check out its reliability? In this manner, we'll be able to cover more ground and prioritise any leads'. Crawford readily agreed with Lizzie's suggestion, 'I will work out a suitable pairing of our forces and talk further on this tomorrow morning.

Crawford slumped into his comfortable leather chair. He felt weary, and Hill's stupidity at Downing Street hadn't helped his composure. He checked his reflection in a nearby mirror; as his likeness came into focus it became apparent to him that he had aged dramatically during the past months. His hair was greyer and thinner, his beard appeared unruly and the lines under his blurry eyes were greatly pronounced. 'This job will be the death of me', he thought. 'Best get home to bed'.

Lizzie was at the office early the next day and enquired if William had any luck browsing his maps. 'Sorry, Miss,' he replied through sleepless eyes. William looked dead on his feet. 'Best go home, William. I'll cover you until the boss gets in'. Crawford arrived shortly after William left the building; he was also impatient to ascertain if Weaver had come up with anything. 'Complete zero', Lizzie replied, 'he was shattered, so I suggested he went home to catch up on lost sleep'.

At nine o'clock, the whole team less William Weaver assembled around Crawford, waiting for instructions. 'I like Lizzie's suggestion of splitting into pairs, and I've written my thoughts in my notebook', which he removed from his pocket and placed on the table. His scribbled notes revealed that his team was sorely undermanned and needed assistance from the local constabulary. It revealed the following plan –

Briggs will be paired with one of Peel's men
Hill and Lizzie will partner each other
Trevaliant will continue with his assignment at Dover
Vickers will be paired with one of Peel's men
Weaver will remain at Whitehall to collate our findings

Crawford heard rumblings of dissatisfaction as his team had taken in their respective pairings.

'Don't push me', he shouted, 'what we do here is bloody important, we're not on a Sunday school outing. Somewhere out there, an arsonist is at work. It's our job to find him. The next time I hear anyone questioning my decisions, I might decide to spill the beans about which of you prefers the company of little boys'. Hill unexpectedly supported Crawford by calming the unruly noise with the sound of his bellowing voice, 'If Mister Crawford hasn't any objections, I suggest each pairing be assigned a specific quadrant within London. Richard could go north, Henry south before continuing his duties at Dover, Samuel west, leaving me and Lizzie to check out the east. Knowing Mister Crawford as I do, I have no doubt he will enjoy a free-reign to go wherever his instincts take him. That just leaves Willie to evaluate our findings. If nothing of significance comes to light, then each team could radiate further afield'. Crawford was pleased, and at the same time stunned by Hill's willingness to please. At long last, the man was making sense, but he wondered how long it would last.

Henry Trevaliant began his investigations south of the river at the Borough Market in Southwark. He hoped the market traders had gossip to impart, along the lines of landlords and barmaids. However, with the exception of some minor criminal activities, nothing of relevance was to be gained around the market area and the surrounding districts.

Lizzie and Lord Hill headed east in the direction of Brick Lane, just north of Whitechapel, but discovering nothing of interest, they promptly moved on to Roman Road and the flower market at Columbia Road. They had extended their search as far as Hackney and Poplar before returning to Whitehall to rethink their tactics. They were the first team to return, arriving shortly after eight in the evening.

Richard walked from tavern to tavern, the first being the Red Lion at Westminster, followed by the Cittie of York, The Mitre at Covent Garden and finally the Lamb near Leadenhall Street. It was not until he reached the outer limits of his designated area that his nose started to twitch.

Meanwhile, Samuel Vickers was checking his allotted western search area, travelling by boat along the banks of the river as far upstream as Brentford and Isleworth. He had briefly stopped to ask questions at the Yorkshire Grey Tavern at Chelsea, the Old Ship at Hammersmith, the Doves at Chiswick, the Bull's Head and the City Barge at Kew before finishing his journey at the London Apprentice at Isleworth. At the end of it, he ordered his waterman to turn his boat around and head back downstream to Westminster. Thankfully, the day was sunny and bright; the waterman was knowledgeable and humorous – apart from that, Samuel's day had been a waste of time.

Richard Briggs arrived at Primrose Hill by early afternoon, and it was his intention to go no further than Hampstead. Richard was particularly interested in a tavern at Hampstead Heath called the Spaniard's Inn, where he arrived shortly before five o'clock. The landlord had endeavoured to increase his trade by grossly exaggerating that the notorious highwayman Dick Turpin regularly frequented his establishment when travelling to and from northern England. There were numerous old faded posters and drawings of Dick Turpin spread evenly about the white-washed walls of the inn, together with old wanted posters dating back to Turpin's era. Briggs doubted the authenticity of the various drawings and prints. As far as he could recall from his time at college, very little was known about Turpin; some even queried if that was his correct name. During his military college days, he remembered checking every police and court file regarding the highwayman. Many witnesses had testified that his true name was Richard Palmer, and that he was a butcher's son from Essex.

Up until the time of his execution, many years ago, everyone believed Turpin was a cruel merciless highwayman responsible for countless murders, many of which had been committed at the same time of day many miles apart. Most of Turpin's supposed exploits were considered highly dubious at best, including his famous feat of riding from London to York in less than twenty hours. Richard knew that most of Turpin's exploits were rubbish, propagated by William Ainsworth's recently published book that, together with fanciful stores retold within the Penny Bloods, later to be renamed Penny Dreadfuls – those cheap fictional publications accompanied by lavished illustrations that were so popular among the uneducated working classes – attributed to Turpin's myth as a romantic highwayman. Richard remembered excitedly reading in his early childhood 'Black Bess or Knight of the Road'. Richard now viewed those books with utter contempt, asking himself why many writers of the day turned monsters into heroic idols. The truth surrounding Black Bess and her famous journey carrying Turpin upon her back was complete rubbish; the story was fabricated on another highwayman named John 'Swift Nick' Nevison, who had robbed a homeward-bound sailor on the road outside Gads Hill in Kent sixty years previous to Turpin's escapades. Nevison urgently needed to establish an alibi, so he travelled from Kent to York, a journey of nearly two hundred miles in under twenty hours, thinking that if he was seen in York he couldn't be accused of a crime in Kent.

It was only at the end of Turpin's violent life, while he waited to be executed at York race-course, that he exhibited any of his swaggering nonchalance, heroism or derring-do that had been supposedly attributed to him. Prior to that, both his existence and criminal ventures had been predominantly unsavoury.

What caught Richard's eye was a poster advertising a street market at Hatfield's Town Square the following Saturday. Hatfield was not very far from Hampstead, probably less than sixteen miles further north in the nearby county of Hertfordshire. Could this be the reference within the coded message, 'a field of hats'? Richard quickly pondered on the connection and was convinced his assumption was right. Not wanting to waste any time, he departed from the Spaniard's Inn to return to Whitehall and update his colleagues on his good fortune, which was a pity as two pints of good ale were waiting for him, courtesy of the landlord.

Richard arrived back at Whitehall past eight o'clock. The rest of the team were already there, discussing the mixed fortunes of their day, but their smiles quickly evaporated due to Crawford's unnaturally aggressive manner. It appeared that during the lunch period, while the office was left temporally unattended, someone had left a note addressed to him. 'The bastard is playing games with us', he shouted.

Crawford finally noticed the arrival of Briggs and asked, more out of hope, 'I trust you have some good news for me? I'm in desperate need of something to brighten my day. It seems our agency is no longer a clandestine operation'. Crawford continued by informing his team, 'We no longer have the benefit of surprise. Our adversary knows we're looking for him'. Lizzie interrupted Crawford by adding a couple of words, 'We might be looking for her', she said.

At last Richard could talk without others in the office muddying the waters. 'I've just returned from Hampstead Heath'. Crawford looked up – Richard had his full attention. 'A few miles further north lies the village of Hatfield', he stated. The entire team was focused on what Richard had just said – Hatfield. Richard quickly outlined his suspicions regarding Hatfield as the likely target for an arson attack, although he failed to understand the importance of such a small village.

Crawford called out to Lizzie, 'Get me a map of Hatfield,' adding the word 'please' after his request. Crawford was a man renowned for being full of fight and fury one minute, followed by calm and tranquillity the next. He was a man who seldom held a grudge, and seldom against a friend or colleague, although he did make exceptions for Lord Hill.

Briggs peered over Crawford's shoulder, muttering into his commander's ear that Hatfield, if that was the target, seemed a most unremarkable place, not much bigger than a village. It had a couple of public houses, one of which was called the Eight Bells in Park Street; although, if he remembered properly, it was once called the Five Bells, and the surrounding countryside was good fertile farming land that had been rented out to numerous tenant farmers for rearing sheep and cattle. Crops of various kinds grew in the lush land, all of which made their way to London during harvest time. 'Hardly a place of political interest,' Hill added.

Crawford swiftly scanned the map Lizzie had provided and asked, 'Has anyone been to Hatfield?' Hill informed Crawford that Queen Elizabeth and King William had spent much of their childhood at Hatfield House. 'It's more of a palace than a house, and remains home to the…', Hill scratched his thick short grey hair trying to remember the name of the occupants. Remembering his own disappointment with stately homes, he no longer held the subject close to his heart. He was endeavouring to recall the owners of Hatfield House, and if it had any political connections when Crawford suddenly supplied the answer.

'It is home to the Salisbury family; the Dowager has been a political fund raiser for the Conservative party'.

'Yes, of course, you're most accurate, thank you, John', Hill slipped away from the team and strolled wearily back to a seat towards the rear of the room, his head full of despair of what might have been. He was thinking about his own estate, inherited from his father, but sadly his father had left him with astronomical debts, and the only way out was to sell his estate, but he had a title. The mention of politicians normally enraged Hill, but at this moment he remained silent in his solitude.

Lizzie enquired about the whereabouts of the coded message sent to Sir Robert Peel. In all the excitement Crawford had clean forgotten about the Prime Minister's note. He handed the message to Lizzie who carefully scrutinised the contents. 'Well, the paper is obviously from the same source as the others, and the message, as before, is written in French. But what confuses me is that our arsonist is fully aware about the fracas both inside and outside Downing Street'. Hill glimpsed up from studying the floor, a slight smile passed his mouth as he recalled the pleasure he felt when forcing Goulburn from his chair.

Lizzie laid the message on the desk for Crawford to translate –

Good day Mister Crawford,

'Quite a performance, o what a show,
To witness your man deliver that blow.
Once inside what have you in store,
Only poor Goulburn crashed to the floor'.

With Trevaliant stationed at Dover, Crawford who had a reasonable knowledge of the French language from his diplomatic days translated the message. After he finished his translation, he gathered his team around the table to speculate on the message's contents. Lizzie was quick to react by stating the obvious. 'The code may have been written in French, but the writer has reverted to poetry to get his message across, and not very good poetry at that. Anyone within the close proximity of Downing Street could have witnessed the disturbance, but to be aware of Henry Goulburn being forcibly removed from his seat, the bastard must have been inside the building; there is no other way he could know about the mêlée'. Lizzie turned to Samuel for support, but, sensing none coming, she turned instead to Richard. 'Unless', Richard hated what he was about to say, 'unless', he repeated to stress his point, 'our arsonist is one of Peel's inner circle of friends'.

Crawford thought about the possibility for some seconds before replying, 'It just doesn't make sense. It seems ridiculous, even traitorous to consider it as a possibility, but I cannot come up with any other option. The fact, my friends, is that besides Hill and me, no one else was present except Sir Robert and his close friends'.

Hill could be over-zealous at times, but no one could ever accuse him of having traitorous feelings. Crawford trusted him with his life. One thing was for sure: Lord Hill was most certainly not a traitor to his country. The only possible explanation had to be that the Prime Minister had an arsonist within his ranks. However, at present and without proof, no one could afford to speculate further on the subject unless they could produce evidence of their suspicions. Crawford feared that if any confirmation had existed it would be nigh impossible to locate now.

Crawford was convinced that Briggs had unearthed the exact location of the next atrocity, but with members of Peel's cabinet to keep tabs on in case any of them were complicit, his team would be stretched very thin. He had to think quickly. 'I'll arrange with Sir Robert for one of you to be employed inside Downing Street; I need ears and eyes inside the place'. He considered sending Hill but before openly mentioning his name he hastily changed his mind by substituting Lizzie for Hill. Crawford couldn't risk another diplomatic row so soon after Hill's last altercation. 'I'll travel to Hatfield to evaluate the place, and David, you will come with me. Richard please remain on standby for my instructions; I need to speak to Peel before allocating you'.

Crawford decided to take the Prime Minister into his confidence by telling him a little 'white-lie'. 'I fear,' Crawford intimated, 'there may be an attempt to kidnap one or more of your ministers. In view of this, I must request you give me full details of all their future movements. However, we mustn't cause any of them to panic; we need to keep this low-key and to insure normality I think it best if we don't alert any of them about what I've just told you; our agency doesn't want to alarm anyone'. Lizzie sarcastically thought Crawford's reasoning to be extremely clever, especially for a man.

With tickets pre-paid by William Weaver, the mail coach from Westminster to Newcastle left shortly after seven in the morning on Saturday the tenth of January. It made its second stop soon after nine-thirty outside the Eight Bells Public House, off Park Street, just off the Great North Road to allow the horses to rest and drink. The coach was able to accommodate six passengers, but that morning, only four had boarded at Westminster, and two of those had disembarked at Hampstead. Crawford and Hill travelled alone to Hatfield, where they disembarked the coach, where three elderly ladies got off to travel onwards to Doncaster. The two men were most pleased that the journey was not overly long – any further and both of them would wonder if certain parts of their anatomy would ever work again. They had always avoided the subject of getting old, but today's excursion had brought their longevity into focus.

Upon standing on firm ground, they stretched their weary muscles and rubbed their stiff legs in a futile attempt to get life back into their aching bodies and to get their blood circulating around their aging frames. Hill smiled as Crawford reminded him that neither of them was as young as they thought they were – neither man would ever see seventy again, just like their old friend Sir Richard Sharpe. What the trio lacked in strength, however, they more than made up in experience and knowledge. They both missed their good friend Richard Sharpe and neither man had heard from him since he returned to his beloved smallholding in France prior to Maynard's wedding.

Hill studied the small village green, but his eyes first scrutinised the Eight Bells, or perhaps it was the two young girls who were beating the dirt out of a couple of old rugs that straddled a strong rope. Hill nudged Crawford gently in the ribs to enquire if this might be the place to rent rooms. Crawford was fully aware of his friend's wandering hands, but the Eight Bells had to be where they should be based as it directly overlooked the main entrance to Hatfield House. For the vast majority of his life, Crawford had been a righteous and God-fearing man, but he frequently had to remind his friend of the Gospel according to Matthew 26:41. Crawford enjoyed teasing his friend especially when his eyes were rolling in their sockets when transfixed on young girls:

'Watch and pray that ye enter not into temptation: the spirit indeed is willing, but the flesh is weak'.

Crawford had considered staying at the Spaniard's Inn at Hampstead, but that would have incurred an hour's ride each day; he therefore had no choice but to rent rooms at the Eight Bells. There was little point in being sixteen miles from his suspected arsonist. Crawford beamed at the landlord, Silas Kefford, and wished him a hearty 'good morning' before enquiring if the two rooms directly above the bar area were available. Silas Kefford seemed puzzled as his guests normally steered well clear of those particular rooms, and for two good reasons – first, due to the noise from the drunken revellers beneath and second, on account of the squeaking, swaying, tavern sign that hung outside between the bedrooms. Crawford discarded both reasons suggesting a little grease would solve one problem, whilst the second would be overcome by the onset of winter. 'I dare say,' Crawford responded, 'many of your customers will stay within the confines of their own homes to enjoy the delights of a good log-burning fire and their loved ones sitting comfortably upon their laps'. Kefford smiled a toothless smile not knowing if Crawford was jesting or not before enquiring, 'How many nights do you intend to stay?' To this, Lord Hill answered, 'At present, we're unsure but we're happy to pay a month's rent in advance to secure the rooms which, I assume, include breakfast and an evening meal'.

Silas Kefford was rubbing his hands in glee; the reply was music to his ears and pockets. 'Normally I charge guineas per week for each room including breakfast and a hearty evening meal, but as we are in January which is a quiet month, I am happy to reduce the charge to just two gold guineas with a change of bed linen every other Monday and a hot tub every other Friday. If we're in agreement shall we shake to complete the deal?' Crawford was happy with the arrangements until Kefford blew excess mucus from his nose, wiped it on the back of his hand and shirt sleeve before extending his hand to Crawford. Kefford felt brazen as he shook Crawford's hand; he detected some form of disapproval, but he assumed this was nothing more than paying over the odds for the upstairs bedrooms.

Kefford carried on with his monotonous well-rehearsed dribble when explaining his house rules – 'Breakfast will be served between seven-thirty and nine o'clock every morning except for Sunday. Being the Lord's Day, I have no doubt you will join us in prayer at our beautiful church; therefore, breakfast on Sundays will be a cold meal served no later than eight-fifteen. Crawford nodded to show his agreement, but Hill thought that breakfast ending at nine o'clock was positively disgraceful, and as for going to the nearby church on Sunday, that had never been in his nature. Hill continued his aggressiveness by adding, 'If the Good Lord wishes to visit me on Sunday morning, he can come visit me in bed, as it is highly probable I will miss breakfast. If he does come, we will both miss breakfast, and the church service'.

Kefford didn't react in retaliation to Hill's abusive tone regarding the act of prayer, but he did try to leave his guests in a more favourable state by informing them that his daughter, Hestia, would personally clean their rooms prior to carrying hot water for their tubs. This despite Crawford telling Kefford not to bother. 'We're both more than capable of carrying hot water up to our rooms'. Hill wondered if his friend was purposely trying to upset him.

'Here's the menu for tonight'. Silas Kefford suggested the roast turkey. Both men appeared satisfied after reading the small chalked board – they had a choice of turkey or lamb. Finally both men ordered the soup, roast turkey with all the trimmings, finishing with apple pie and cream.

Silas left the bar after wishing his guests a pleasant day, before returning to his cellars to bottle-up for the day's trade. Hestia had been standing by her father's side throughout the booking and meal procedure. As her father vanished into the cellar, she disappeared into the kitchen to help her mother. 'Hestia, lovely name, don't you agree, John?' But Crawford didn't bother to respond during Hill's pointless conversations. They were here for a job, not to make friends with the locals.

Hill and Crawford remained seated in the small bar area of the Eight Bells, Kefford had as yet not offered either man their keys. As he returned from the cellar, he enquired, 'I know it's a bit early in the day but do either of you good gentlemen wish a pint of Hertford ale?' Hill was most happy to accept the offer of ale, but Crawford was impatient to unpack and asked for his room key. Kefford informed his guests that no one else would be staying at the Eight Bells until after the weekend, so peace and quiet would be assured.

'We can all certainly do with that Mister Kefford', and with a final wave Crawford and Hill climbed the stairs to inspect their rooms. They were sparsely furnished, but the important thing was that the bedding was clean.

Silas Kefford, Master of the House

CHAPTER 4

As Sober as a Judge

Vickers sent regular communications to Crawford's care off Silas Kefford at the Eight Bells. Hill was deeply suspicious of Kefford; he didn't trust the man and worried constantly if he had intercepted or opened any letters marked confidential, but Crawford wasn't overly bothered, he never asked awkward questions of his landlord and always considered him a jovial if not a simplistic character, who was always the first to greet him with a pleasant 'good morning,' or 'good afternoon'. What was more, his evening meals were of a good quality and particularly well cooked; anyone who served meals of this quality must be trustworthy. Crawford had again eaten breakfast alone – Hill hadn't managed to get out of bed before nine to eat breakfast or attend the Sunday church service. By the beginning of the second week, Lord Hill had only managed to make one solitary breakfast appearance, if you counted tea and toast as breakfast; the rest of the week he preferred to remain in bed for that extra hour.

Crawford was excited when his pre-ordered edition of Mister Charles Dickens' first novel, The Pickwick Papers was delivered to the Eight Bells, and he hoped to pass any free time he got with pleasurable reading. So far, nothing out of the ordinary had occurred. Lord Hill was swiftly flipping his way through The Times to inform his companion of any snippets he considered interesting. There was an article concerning the recent arson attacks at the Heckingham Workhouse in Norfolk, but Crawford dismissed this and other assaults on workhouses in the Norfolk area as being nothing more than the work of a disgruntled mob and not the work of an evil bastard intent on killing and setting fires for his own personal gratification. Hill interrupted Crawford's thinking by reminding his boss that 'according to Lizzie the bugger might be a female'. 'Lizzie doesn't know everything', Crawford responded somewhat ironically.

Hill carried on flipping through the pages. 'This is interesting', he said, feeling angry and bitter, 'An interesting article appertaining to a new horserace. The first race will be run over unusually big fences at a place called Aintree in Lancashire'. Hill held the page closer to Crawford to assist his reading. 'They intend to call the race the Grand National Steeplechase, and for some stupid reason they intend to hold the meet near Liverpool'. Crawford looked surprised as he glared at Hill, who looked him straight in the face. 'What's the problem with Liverpool?' 'The bloody place is full of Irish'. Crawford sighed to himself as he tried to keep the conversation going, 'If it ain't bankers, lawyers or politicians, my friend, you now apparently hold a grudge against the poor Irish. Whatever have the Irish done to you, David?' He wished he hadn't asked the question when his friend gave his bigoted answer, 'Well, for a start, there's too many of the buggers; they breed like rabbits! Then, when their potato crops fail, which they invariably do, they hold their grubby little hands out for government relief'.

Crawford felt enormous sympathy for the Irish. Through no fault of their own, their crops failed again, infected by a fungus type, blight. Hill continued with his unwarranted attack on the Irish. 'Mark my words, John, one day there will be more Irish living around the world than in their native land'.

A change of subject was required. 'Besides bloody horse-racing and the Irish, is there anything else in your newspaper regarding arson or murders?' Crawford curtly enquired. Hill returned to check through the headlines and quickly flipped through the flimsy pages. 'A chap named Daniel Case from Ilchester has been hanged for starting fires'. Crawford dismissed the article with a wave of his hand as having no relevance to their enquiries. With the exception of that single report, the newspaper was void of any other arson attacks. Murders, on the other hand, were common place; too many, in Crawford's view, for most of them to become headline news.

'Nothing in the newspaper except the continual bickering between Whig and Tory, Melbourne and Peel, which, I fear, our old friend Melbourne seems to be winning'.

Hill glanced up from his newspaper and smilingly informed Crawford, 'Damn politics, that's all they print about these days, although I see they've moved the Oxford-Cambridge University boat race from Henley to a new starting point near Westminster Bridge. It says here that your old university

Cambridge were the victors by over twenty lengths – that should put a smile on your face, John'. It did, but Crawford didn't let his friend see it.

Without any useful leads to go by, Crawford became acutely aware of the whims of politicians. If they could initiate a secret diplomatic agency, they could just as easily kill it off.

Noticing his friend's unease, Hill offered Crawford a glimmer of encouragement, 'Sooner or later this fucking arsonist will make a big mistake, and rest assured, when he does, we'll be on hand to seize the bastard; I take it there has been nothing of interest from our surveillance teams?' Without looking up, Crawford sighed, 'Sadly, none'.

The year ended relatively calm, and the people hoped the new year would bring similar cheer; however, unbeknown to everyone, dramatic changes were looming on the horizon.

In January, Sir Robert was forced to call another general election, the result of which brought Melbourne's opposition party within touching distance of outright victory. A small swing of fifteen seats and victory would have been Melbourne's, but what made matters worse was that it was plainly evident that the King preferred Peel's counsel. The country was convinced that whenever the next election came, it would bring far-reaching reforms heralding a new chapter in English politics. Whilst waiting for his opportunity, Melbourne appointed Lord John Russell as his new shadow home secretary, Palmerston as his shadow foreign secretary, Thomas

Spring Rice as his shadow chancellor, Lord Gleneig as his shadow secretary for war, and Charles Poulett Thomas as his shadow president of the board of trade. Crawford was concerned about these appointees having traitorous tendencies. He wanted to ignore the facts, but he dared not; someone had written a coded letter confirming something that they should not have witnessed. Crawford had to be guarded!

In addition to the Murphy world of politics, the new year brought unforeseen changes to the Crown. King William's short reign ended on the twentieth day of June when the so-called 'Sailor King', while residing at Windsor Castle, died at the age of seventy-one due to a massive heart attack, two days after the celebration of the battle of Waterloo – it was thought that the King's drinking habits of downing more than one bottle of sherry per day may have contributed to his demise. His successor to the throne of Great Britain and Ireland had been announced as Princess Alexandrina of Kent, the only child of Prince Edward, Duke of Kent, and his wife, Princes Victoria of Saxe-Coburg-Saalfeld. The princess, a niece of the late King, was a young girl of eighteen years and one month, a significant fact, as William was heard to state in the year prior to his death, 'I trust God that my life may be spared for nine months longer, I should then have the satisfaction of leaving the exercise of the Royal authority to the personal authority of that young lady, heiress presumptive to the Crown, and not in the hands of a person now near me, who is surrounded by evil advisors and is herself incompetent to act with propriety in the situation in which she would be placed'. On hearing the news of the King's death,

Crawford sat cross-armed at the breakfast table, contemplating all the good work the King had the forethought to instigate.

Hill, on the other hand, true to form, found it difficult to accept a young girl, who had little or no experience in life, as his Queen. However, for some reason, he seemed much happier when Princess Alexandrina selected her middle name for her forthcoming coronation. Hill turned to Crawford and stated rather unexpectedly, 'I rather like this young woman – Victoria has a much better ring to it. I suspect the country is about to regain much of the splendour and magnificence of its former years; we might well be in for another golden age'.

Crawford glared at Hill in amazement, as if he was a spoilt child. 'You surprise me at times, David, with the triviality of your line of reasoning'. It was all very well for Hill to reminisce about former glories, but he had to constantly remind himself not to forget the purpose of why they were here. 'We're supposed to be keeping our eyes and ears wide open to the comings and goings on at the big house. I have little doubt that something will happen, but as to when and by whom I don't as yet know'. Crawford glanced at his friend. 'Unless you have taken up fortune telling, that is still our objective'.

Following Melbourne's electoral success in April, Weaver sent a message to Crawford explaining that Russell and Palmerston would attend a conference in Dublin to discuss the year's potato famine, which the newly elected Prime Minister predicted could result in a mass exodus from Ireland –

Crawford decided to keep that information to himself, thinking it best not to share some things with Hill. Thomas Rice, as chancellor, would be working on his new budget which, he hoped would be ready before the autumn statement, while Lord Gleneig and Charles Thomas had been dispatched to France to discuss renewing trade arrangements between France and England with the French Prime Minister, Louis-Mathieu Molé.

Crawford was deeply concerned about the prospects of having to assign three surveillance teams with only three officers at his disposal, bearing in mind that he had already lost Trevaliant to the cross-channel port of Dover. All he had at his disposal were Richard, Samuel, Lizzie and Willie, but William was not a field operative – he had no experience. He called Hill to his room to discuss tactics and whom to send where. After much consideration, Briggs was sent to Dublin, Lizzie to Downing Street and Samuel to France, leaving William in relative safety at Whitchall. 'That's all we can do, John'.

Towards the end of October, Russell and Palmerston were in Dublin, closely followed by Richard Briggs, who had reserved a room at the Ormond Quay Hotel at Bloomsday, and Lizzie Drew was not so comfortable with washing dishes as a kitchen maid's duties at number eleven Downing Street required. Sam Vickers sailed to France with Lord Palmerston as part of his entourage; the delegation had booked into the luxurious Four Seasons Hotel close to the intersection with the Avenue George V and the Avenue Pierre 1st er de Serbie. Crawford hated the idea of Lizzie being used as a kitchen servant at Downing Street. As she was his god-daughter, he knew she would have words next time they met.

William Weaver was assigned to keep guard over the Whitehall office, where Crawford hoped regular reports would be filtered by him before he passed them on to him at Hatfield. Intelligence slowly came to William indicating that Rice had arranged bedrooms for his aids, which meant his budget would take some time before being completed. In addition, as every home comfort had been laid on for Rice and his small team of financial advisors, nobody had a reason to leave number eleven – the only comings and goings were the chandlers delivering food and drink. Only the regular household staff had permission to leave the building, and as Lizzie wasn't a regular member of staff, she was excluded from this privilege.

Rice's budget was proving extremely difficult to calculate; it seemed nearly impossible to balance the books without hurting someone. Lizzie overheard the chancellor talking to his advisors about his thoughts on reintroducing income tax, but his advisors pulled him back from the brink by forcibly explaining to Rice that this unpopular tax would in truth only hurt Viscount Melbourne's supporters. In addition, income tax only affected those earning more than £150 per annum – the very people who had voted Melbourne into office.

Hill was looking forlorn; the lack of breakfast was not agreeing with his constitution. On the other hand, Crawford had no trouble adjusting his body-clock to accommodate the first meal of the day, even at eight in the morning. On most mornings, Lord Hill overlooked breakfast, but there were the odd occasions when he did manage to sit down with Crawford with barely five minutes to spare, by which time his friend had usually finished his third pot of tea. Crawford joked – much to Hill's annoyance – about how good the helpings of bacon, sausage, toast, eggs, black pudding and fried tomatoes tasted.

'Why don't you retire earlier in the evening David? This will greatly improve your manners first thing in the morning, and after savouring the taste of Misses Kefford's delicious cooking, you will be set for the day – trust me!'

Hill chugged a cup of steaming hot over-brewed tea down his gullet before banging his cup on the table to signify that he wished Silas to re-fill his cup. Hill simply disregarded Crawford's friendly advice, much to his annoyance.

'How the hell did you manage to reach the lofty title of Lord, David?' Crawford asked more out of anger than inquisitiveness, 'You're losing weight, you can't expect to keep your wits about you while continuing to forgo breakfast prepared by our host's wife'. Hill glanced up at his friend and, putting his hands together as though mimicking as prayer, said, 'Here endeth the first lesson – have we finished?'

Hill wiped his mouth with the cuff of his jacket, belched loudly before uttering his first words of the day, or the words he repeated every morning since their arrival at Hatfield – 'What's on the agenda today?' followed by, 'Don't tell me another ramble through the woods pretending to watch birds'.

Evidently Lord Hill was not keen on bird watching!

When Hill was in a bad mood, God help anybody who stood in his way. He quickly transformed from being one of Crawford's closest friends into a grumpy old git. Surely missing breakfast couldn't be the sole reason for his irrational behaviour, but evidently it was!

The weather had changed. Instead of the damp foggy mornings, the rain fell in buckets. That should have cheered Hill, as it meant they couldn't go out that morning seeking rare birds on such as horrific day. Crawford opened the curtains to peer out; it was raining so hard that his line of vision couldn't extend more than fifty yards. Crawford was visibly upset, but Hill appeared content.

'Have any newspapers arrived yet'? Hill shouted over to Kefford, 'And what's the chances of another pot of tea'. Silas confirmed that the papers had just been delivered, and he would bring them over to his guests together with the tea. 'Why don't you bring another chair with you Silas? I'm in need of local gossip this morning'.

Kefford explained that nowadays, the Dowager Marchioness, the First Lady Salisbury, travelled from her London residence to spend Christmas and the New Year at Hatfield House. 'Her son and his family had tried to tempt the old dear to spend the holiday season in the South of France, but she would hear none of it. She didn't like breaking with tradition'. 'When will they arrive?' Crawford asked, 'They already have', replied Silas, 'Got here about ten days ago with her son, daughter-in-law and grand-children'.

'Already arrived... that's strange', Crawford retorted, 'I've not seen any coaches entering or leaving Hatfield House since we got here'.

'That's because they entered via the entrance on the south side. The family don't like to make a fuss', Silas responded. 'The Dowager is a friendly old girl, well over eighty so she is. We villagers affectionately call her 'Old Sally' – don't know why though. In her younger says, she took an avid interest in our village life. She once entered my humble tavern to buy a round of drinks for the locals to celebrate Wellington's victory at Waterloo. If I remember correctly, she purchased a drop of whisky for everyone on account of the severe weather in the summer of 1815. Her Ladyship enjoyed a drink in those days, but of late she has abstained from alcohol on account of her age. She was always popular with the villagers, never was one who put on her airs and graces, not like others I can mention! Her old man, His Lordship, passed away over ten years ago. In her heyday, Old Sally was very much what you might call a trendsetter. She loved to wear outrageous costumes which she designed herself. We locals regularly saw her out hunting, wearing a sky-blue riding habit with a black collar and cuffs along with a silly hunting cap perched high above her head. After her husband's death, the hounds were retired back to the grounds of

Hatfield House, and I assume some might still be there to this very day. These days, her Ladyship has taken up archery, not that her eye-sight allows her to shoot straight. The Dowager keeps herself to herself, although in her day she was a beauty, a diamond that stood out from the crowd'.

Crawford knew of the Dowager Marchioness, not personally, only from political gossip. She was a Tory party supporter and fundraiser and regularly entertained party members to Hatfield House. 'I'll keep that to myself, best not tell Hill'. Crawford always steered well clear of political gossip when Hill was about. Everyone in politics knew Hill had an abrasive tongue but, following his recent antics at Downing Street and his ejection of Russell from his chair, meant invitations to parties had greatly diminished. Crawford and Hill were like chalk and cheese – they say opposites attract, and there couldn't be another combination as far apart as Crawford and Hill. One had been a trusted diplomat working for King and Country; the other had inherited debts and a title. Although Crawford feared that Hill already had debts prior to his father's demise – but friends they were, and friends they would stay! Hill had too many rough edges to his character – he bordered on the extremities of bigotry, while Crawford only looked for fairness, unless the contrary was proved.

'Tell me Silas', Crawford enquired of Kefford, 'Exactly how many entrances are there for Hatfield House?' Silas awkwardly protruded his spindly fingers to assist his counting before answering, 'Lots, but only three that would allow a coach and horses'. Lord Hill glared at Crawford in utter disgust, 'You should have spent more time in the woods counting roads and footpaths instead of watching bloody birds'. If looks could kill, Hill was dead and buried!

'How many people are up at the big house now?' Crawford continued despite Hill's venomous tongue. Once again Kefford made use of his fingers to calculate his answer, 'Two coaches arrived on Tuesday with about five passengers on board, three coaches on Wednesday, but I'm unsure of the number of passengers, and only the single coach arrived yesterday with about three or four ladies on board. The servants were brought up from London the month before to air and clean the house. I can only guess, but I believe the number already in the house must be in excess of fifty'.

'And you missed every one of them, John', Hill exclaimed with great annoyance. 'Remember the old saying about shutting the stable door after the horse has bolted? Well, let's reverse that saying... you left the hen-house door open to allow the fox in – to do his killing before locking the bloody door when he left'.

Crawford reacted with an ugly frown on his face, 'That doesn't make any sense, and well you know it. Go and make yourself scarce while I try to formulate some kind of plan'.

Hill marched out the room in revulsion; he hadn't cocked-up, but he knew who did. 'I bet he doesn't have any plan in his head', he said, still in his resentful mood.

'I need to come up with something pretty quickly', Crawford thought to himself. He knew his strategy was in disarray, but how was he to overcome his blunder? That was how a good leader should instantly react when his original proposal had been blown out of the water. When the shit hit the door, he was the one who had to clean up the mess – not Hill, who had never cleaned his own shit, let alone anyone else's. That was why he was the enforcer and Crawford was in command.

Crawford reluctantly decided to step outside. 'Sod the weather' he muttered. Even though the rain had temporary stopped, the ground was muddy underfoot. He carefully walked to the centre of the village green and casually slumped against an old oak tree; although the bark was damp, it instantly relieved his aching back. Crawford was desperate; he needed something to restore order in his life, or, at the very least, to demonstrate to his companion that he could overcome any of life's difficulties. 'I suppose that great big waste of space has sulked back to the bar to down a wee dram of whisky'.

Crawford knew he had made an error of judgement in failing to realise Hatfield House had multiple entrances. He should have checked the plans for the house before arriving; no doubt every pathway would be clearly marked. Crawford glanced up from his melancholy mood; someone was walking up the main drive, through the ornate gates up to the house – it was Silas Kefford. Crawford called after Kefford, 'Silas', he called his name again – 'Silas!'. Kefford turned slightly, alarmed at hearing his name. 'Good day Mister Crawford, I hadn't seen you there'. Silas waited for his guest to catch up with him; once the two men were standing side by side, Crawford politely enquired where Kefford was going.

'Up to the big house, Mister Crawford', Silas replied, 'I 'ave to make sure they're well stocked with provisions and alcohol, as well as disposing of all the empty casks and bottles'. 'Would you like some company, Mister Kefford?' Crawford graciously asked. Kefford couldn't see any reason to object to Crawford's request, and the two men strolled together towards Hatfield House.

'How often do you carry out this type of duty, Mister Kefford?' Crawford respectfully enquired. 'Normally twice a week, but as there are lots of guests this time of year, I do my best to come up thrice a week. 'Interesting', Crawford thought, as he attempted to formulate a new plan inside his head. 'I 'ave to make sure they are well stocked – can't 'ave empty pantries or empty wine cellars this time of year Mister Crawford, Christmas won't be long in coming', Kefford continued. 'I don't normally come this way but as I was delayed chatting to our local constable, I decided to make up time by walking this way. You can see how the paths split up ahead – I take the left pathway which leads me directly to the servants' quarters. That's where we 'umble tradesmen make our appearances. O I nearly forgot, Kefford continued, 'the constable left a couple of letters for you and the other gentleman'.

Crawford swiftly offered his apologies and dashed back to the Eight Bells, where his scolded companion was reading the local newspaper, with a half full whisky glass close by his right hand. Lord Hill never liked to be reprimanded, so he didn't glance up as Crawford came running through the inn. Hill remained in his belligerent mood as Crawford shouted, 'I think I've found a way of retrieving the situation without losing face. Where have you put the letters that the local Bobbie delivered this morning?'

Hill glanced up from his newspaper and enquired what his friend was on about, 'I didn't propagate any mess. I think you'll find it was you who messed up, and your letters are on your bedside table'.

Crawford dashed up the stairs, two at a time. 'I hope it's good news', but sadly his optimism was cruelly cut short. He walked back downstairs with a letter in each hand. Crawford's guise had changed from high expectation to one of low esteem; he had taken on the appearance of a high court judge about to pronounce a sentence on the accused.

'Tell me, David. What the hell do you make of these'?

CHAPTER 5

Death Pays a Visit

Thankfully the Eight Bells was void of customers as Hill read the first letter. It contained various reports from Dublin, principally from Richard Briggs, who explained that as nothing of significance had been discerned, he was asking if he should terminate his mission and return forthwith to London. He had been in Dublin for nearly five months and the negotiations appeared to be close to finalisation. Briggs was exceedingly worried about wasting time and the tax payer's money on what appeared to be a fruitless task – keeping an eye on individuals who did not appear to be any longer a legitimate target.

Hill glanced at Crawford for a sign of approval or rejection of Briggs suggestions, but seeing neither, he set about reading the second letter; 'Bloody hell, John! I might have guessed, you better just read it to me. You know I have never fully mastered the French language'.

'All those years living in France and you failed to speak like a native', Crawford was getting frustrated by Hill's negativity, 'You amaze me, David'.

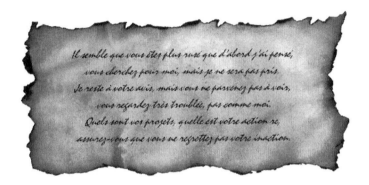

Crawford translated the letter for his friend,

'It seems you are more cunning than first I thought,
You seek for me, but I will not be caught.
I remain in your view, but you fail to see,
You look very troubled, not like me.
What are your plans, what's your re-action?
Make sure you don't regret any inaction'.

'Well, it seems you were right about Hatfield House all along, but why is he taunting us? That's a puzzle to me. I just don't get it! Does he want to be caught?' Hill questioned. Both men fell silent as Misses Kefford started washing tables in the bar; she only remained a few minutes before disappearing back into the kitchen. Crawford thought Kefford's wife was just being nosey, before renewing his conversation, 'Some criminals love to taunt their pursuers; it makes them feel superior. They try to convince themselves and us that they're invincible. They also think their intellect is far superior to ours, but in taunting us the way they do, they make mistakes, or sometimes we make the mistake. It's like a game of hawk-dove to see who blinks first, us or them'.

'So who's the hunted, and who's the hunter? Hill asked.

What worried Crawford more than anything else was that this arsonist had spied on them inside the woods; he was mocking Crawford by explaining he was in plain sight but couldn't be seen by them. 'Where has he been spying on us?' Hill asked somewhat cautiously, 'In the countryside or here at the Eight Bells? If he writes poetry for us, he might even have spoken to us whilst we have lodged here!'

'Don't forget John, Lizzie told us that there could be two arsonists working in unison – the poet might be a woman'. Hill suddenly had a thought, one that Crawford had already considered, 'Could they be husband and wife?'

Crawford wondered who was tracking whom. 'Do you remember the time when Sir Richard disguised himself as an old disabled soldier begging outside the gates of St. Katharine's Dock, east of London, spying on suspects?' Hill nodded, 'I remember it well, especially when Sharpe got drenched. The rain fell hard as nails on that day. Poor Richard…'

With their earlier argument forgotten, Hill realised that he had pushed his friend too far. Although no words were exchanged, Crawford glanced at Hill and knew what his friend was thinking. Very slowly and systematically, he nodded his head in agreement, 'Right, let's get Briggs up here, no time to lose'.

As November approached, the weather turned much colder, but thankfully the rain held off. On the twenty-third of November, Richard Briggs arrived at Hatfield; Crawford and Hill greeted him enthusiastically, treating him like a long-lost brother. Richard was introduced to Silas Kefford, who went through his well-rehearsed rigmarole of explaining the house rules regarding breakfast and dinner times. Kefford failed to mention the offer of changing the bed sheets as part of his package until he noticed Hill's menacing eye scrutinizing him, which released him from his temporary memory loss.

That evening the three friends reminisced past adventures. They all recalled that bloody day in June 1815 when all of them had thought that God was on the verge of taking them, but thanks to Blucher and his Prussians, it was proved that God had other duties for John Crawford. By nine-thirty, Hill and Briggs were under the influence of the Devil's punch-bowl, sliding from their chairs before crawling back into them again. Crawford watched on as the two men poured quart after quart down their gullets; they were now uncontrollably savouring the exaggerated glories of single-handedly clutching victory from despair. Both men were attracting unwelcoming glances from the locals; Crawford initially considered getting both men upstairs to sleep off their excesses, but he suddenly thought he could use his drunken friends over zealous idiocy to his own advantage. What better way of mocking their enemy than to create a carefree triumphant atmosphere, make the bastard think they were near to celebrating his early incarceration. 'More drinks, Landlord!' Crawford shouted to Kefford, 'We'll soon be out of your humble tavern and back to London'. Crawford was happy that his enlarged – albeit by one – pack of hounds would soon snare his quarry. If their tormentor was within the confines of these four walls, he certainly didn't make himself known. The villagers simply accepted the city folk as arrogant fools. He hoped the arsonist was inside the Eight Bells, but he couldn't be sure. Perhaps Lizzie's mind-reading talents could give them an advantage by unlocking the secrets hidden deep inside their brains, make them reveal themselves and confess. But Lizzie was in London washing dishes and was probably hating it.

By ten-thirty, Crawford had had enough. 'You've both had enough drink – time for bed'. Hill thought about arguing the point, but faintly recalling his earlier upset with Crawford, he decided he and Briggs should retire – but not before ordering large brandies for both of them as a night-cap. Hill staggered over to the bar, leaving Briggs asleep where he had fallen on the floor. 'Misses Kefford, my sweet, can I order two brandies to take to bed with me?' Julia Kefford was taken aback by her guest's overfamiliarity, but put his intimacy down to the demon drink. She poured two large brandies and smiled at her guest; the poor man was having trouble standing. If it hadn't been for the counter supporting his limp arms, he would be unconscious on the floor. 'Good night, my Lord, and sleep well'. She put her rosy red lips to his forehead as she spoke those finishing words. She kissed him as a mother would kiss her child. Before Hill could react to Julia's sweet kiss, in pain he crashed on one knee. He thought he might either pass out or vomit. The last thing he remembered rattling inside his drunken head was Crawford telling him, 'The spirit indeed is willing, but the flesh is weak'. Silas Kefford, John Crawford, and a couple of the villagers were left to carry two highly inebriated fools up to bed.

Crawford was very surprised when he was the last to arrive at the breakfast table. It was just before eight o'clock and Hill and Briggs were already enjoying their hearty breakfasts. 'You look well, David. A good night's sleep appears to have ironed out those large bags from under your eyes'. Bearing in mind the early hour, Hill surprisingly did look well, but Richard Briggs looked as if every mouthful was torment. Two minutes later, he headed outside to unceremoniously regurgitate his breakfast. 'Not like us, John', Hill laughed, 'We can take it; these youngsters cannot'. Briggs giggled as he rejoined the breakfast table, wondering what Hill was thinking about this early in the morning. He waited for any adverse reaction to his momentary dash to relieve his stomach of its contents, but when Hill did nothing, he glanced sheepishly at Crawford before smirking back at Lord Hill, who suddenly burst into laughter,

90

spitting bits of sausage and egg all over the cloth covering the breakfast table. 'You will learn one day Richard not to try and drink me under the table', before gently poking his hung-over friend in the ribs, triggering an additional outburst of unruly merriment and gaiety.

Crawford appealed for calm while he caught up with his own breakfast. From that moment onwards, he knew he was the undisputed leader of the team. He recalled one particular line from a Shakespeare comedy—

'Some are born great, some achieve greatness, and some have greatness thrust upon them', he softly whispered to himself.

'Twelfth Night', Briggs whispered back.

'What?' replied Crawford.

'The comedy, the line you just mentioned, it's from Twelfth Night'. 'So it is', Crawford happily answered. Briggs might not be a drinker, but he knew his Shakespeare!

That line from Twelfth Night reverberated inside his head, and his brain kept replying to him – 'Some have greatness thrust upon them'. That was exactly how he thought of himself – he hadn't sought command, but command had thrust itself upon him.

'Now that we are three, I think we might be able to keep watch from additional vantage points'. Crawford thought it best if Hill and Briggs remained out of sight the next time he strolled up to the big house with Silas Kefford. That way, his two colleagues could keep him under surveillance. 'The watchers watching the watcher', he said to himself.

Silas and Julia Kefford cleared the mess away from the breakfast table, and while Briggs and Hill retired outside to smoke their clay pipes, Crawford got the opportunity to speak to Silas alone. 'Tell me, Mister Kefford', Crawford enquired, 'When are you next due to attend the big house?' 'I should go back this afternoon, Mister Crawford', Kefford volunteered, 'There are many empty casks, wine and beer bottles to bring back'. 'That being the case, have you any objection to me accompanying you? We can get the job done in half the time. I get so bored wandering around the countryside in search of the illusive Wryneck Woodpecker. It seems the bird doesn't want my company, so I am at your disposal'. Kefford rubbed the mousy coloured stubble on his chin, before brushing back the long unkempt hair away from the front of his face. 'I don't see any 'arm in that, sir', Kefford eventually replied, as he cuffed excess spittle from his mouth before spewing the rest onto the tavern floor. Crawford turned away in disgust, as he couldn't abide such displays of abhorrent crudeness. Kefford blew his nose on a piece of dirty old rag, which instead of throwing away he stuffed back inside his waistcoat pocket. 'See you in the kitchen at one o'clock, Mister Crawford'.

'I'll be there, Mister Kefford', Crawford responded.

At precisely one o'clock, the two men ambled toward the big house. They strolled along the main path leading past the magnificent circular fountain before veering off to the left as before. Due to the freezing temperature, the mountain had been switched off and lay still with fallen winters leaves covering its surface. The two men guided the cart to a small doorway, evidently the entrance to the kitchens. As they reached the door, a small man clad in a fancy dress exited; he looked embarrassed, explaining to Kefford, whom he evidently knew, that the family were playing charades in the dining room. The servant ushered both men hurriedly into the kitchen, where most of the kegs and bottles were stored. Kefford wanted to be in and out of the house before dark and set about his task with great urgency, but Crawford's eyes were alert to everything. He continually made mental notes regarding what door went where and the number of passageways. The house was a labyrinth of bricks, wood and mortar. Kefford was too busy collecting bottles and empty casks and kegs to notice where Crawford had wandered off. Hatfield House was enormous; it had so many corridors, rooms and hallways that one could easily get lost. He glanced through a partially opened door and stared in disbelief at the sheer size of the highly decorated dining hall. Large amounts of gold and silk adorned the walls of the room. High windows ran along the entire length of the room with perfectly positioned expensive carpets underfoot, some of which partially obscured the black and white mosaic floor. The room could have doubled as a Masonic temple. Crawford continued with his unscheduled viewing, glancing up at the painted ceiling in awe. It was obvious that whoever had commissioned this house had money, and lots of it.

They must have had favour in high places. The building was far too grand for a rich merchant to gratify; the property had nobility written all over it. To Crawford's eyes, the house was not a dwelling; it was a place of regal beauty. It was without a doubt a palace fit for Royalty, just as Lord David Hill had described it.

Crawford was brought back to reality with a start when Kefford gently touched his shoulder. 'Time to leave, Mister Crawford. We're finished here'.

The cart was fully loaded with empty bottles and kegs. Kefford double checked the restraining ropes and the stability of the cart before steering the handcart away from Hatfield House and back to the Eight Bells. As they walked away, Crawford couldn't be inspired by the sheer beauty of the house and thought about the impossible task of protecting the residents should an arsonist attempt to carry out his deadly task. He only had himself and two men under his control; an army of men wouldn't be able to guarantee the safety of everyone inside. He turned back to take one final look at the impressive structure and noted a curtain being manhandled on the upper floor. Crawford turned away to ensure that the cart hadn't strayed onto the manicured lawn before taking a second look at the moving curtain. He had a gut feeling that whoever was checking their departure was not simply idling away the day checking on the scenery or tidying curtains. His guts were seldom wrong; they had served him well, and on numerous occasions, had kept him alive. Intuition or sixth sense was ringing alarm bells inside his brain. Lizzie would know the signs, he thought. Crawford knew Hill and Briggs were somewhere behind him, keeping a watch on him, but was there another sinister observer inside the woods with them?

As they neared the Eight Bells, Crawford heard a loud cry for help and footsteps coming up fast behind on the gravel pathway. He swiftly turned to witness Hill stumbling along, near to exhaustion, no more than twenty feet behind. Both Briggs and Hill were supposed to be acting as a rearguard to make sure he and Kefford returned safely. His instructions to both men was to remain at a distance and not let anyone see them; if Hill had broken cover it could only mean one thing – trouble!

'What's the problem?' Crawford shouted, but Hill was close to collapse, shaking uncontrollably, and he fought to inhale precious air. Kefford and Crawford waited for Hill to catch up; he looked in a bad way as he doubled-over on all fours, fighting to retain consciousness, unable to express himself while he gasped for breath. It was a good two minutes before Hill was able to speak, but then it was only in short bursts, as he needed large intakes of life-saving oxygen between each syllable.

'I heard...a cry...for...help...thought it was Briggsy...but...I couldn't...see...through the...trees...' Hill was in an appalling state; he wasn't making too much sense. As he spluttered out the individual words, his face was bright red and his eyes were near to popping out of his head in pain. He was sweating profusely as he fell from his dog-like position, rolling on his face prostrated. For the time being, he lay powerless to describe what he heard or thought he heard. 'Take it easy', Crawford tried to calm his friend, but Hill would hear none of it as he re-tried to valiantly tell his story. 'I heard Richard...calling for help...he sounded as if...he was suffering'. 'You need to rest. Take short breaths, and relax', Crawford ordered. 'Relax be buggered, Richard is in trouble...I tried to find him...but the lack of day-light was hampering me'. Hill was inconsolable and not making too much sense.

'Have you a drop of brandy in your hip flask, John?' 'Crafty bugger', Crawford thought, 'managed to get that out'.

Kefford had remained silent and open mouthed in alarm as he heard Hill trying to give his account. 'Do you want me to go back for your friend, Mister Crawford'? 'That's unnecessary, Silas. Once Lord Hill has his wits about him, we'll go back and search the woods for our colleague', Crawford advised. 'It will soon be dark'. Kefford had a unique way of explaining the obvious, but Crawford recommended he go back to the Eight Bells. 'We'll be back shortly'.

'But I know them woods better than either of you gentlemen. I can retrace our footsteps all the way back to the house. I know all the paths, it will be quicker for me to search than you, Mister Crawford'. 'Sorry Silas, Richard is our friend. Once Lord Hill regains his composure, we'll go back to seek out his disappearance, *if* he has disappeared'.

Hill's breathing returned to near normal, or as normal as an over-weight, seventy-plus-year-old could be. Crawford assisted his friend to his feet before walking back in the direction they had so recently sauntered. They hurried back along the gravel path for fifteen minutes before Hill tersely came to a halt. He glimpsed tenuously around at his surroundings as if trying to seek out where Richard's last cries for help were heard; to their right, a distinct hollow in the landscape could easily be seen, surrounded by dense scrub and thick prickly bushes, towards the horizon a giant row of poplars stood like colossal sentinels in the murky twilight. The hostile, constantly changing, panorama evoked ghostly sensations within his mind as the swirling wind began to taint the uncanny scenery in the semi-darkness between day and night, inducing strange shadows within the forest. The moon began sharing its paranormal unnatural light with the remnants of the fading sun that had partially dipped under the distant horizon, as if being sucked into earth's grave. On their right, the ground rose steadily to form an impenetrable zenith of ivy, waving on the wind beckoning the unwary into its black heart. In the fading light, the ground seemed to be alive as it suffocated all within its wake. The leafless trees took on the appearance of giant statues slowly being strangled by the sinister mishmash of vile assassins in the shape of spreading ivy and strangling vines. Everything of beauty had been overshadowed by the callous and uncompromising slaughterer within nature's world, leaving in its stead grotesque disfigured relics of decency. The woodland was quiet, maybe too silent. The birds had stopped singing, and no nocturnal creatures could be seen scurrying about the undergrowth in search of food, but the woods were alive with something – something intimidating and sinister.

The two men felt their way through the undergrowth, being especially careful to remain in full sight of each other, reassuringly calling out each other's name. With naught to see or hear, they decided to widen their search perimeter; however, the lack of light hampered their search. Crawford sought to calm Hill's frayed nerves by suggesting that Briggs had probably taken another path back to the pub, and while they were searching the clammy undergrowth, he was enjoying his second or third pint of Kefford's ale. But despite Crawford's feasible reassurance, Hill would hear none of it – he remained adamant and unconvinced by Crawford's appeasement.

'He must me here somewhere; it's just that we haven't found him yet!' Hill knew that without the benefit of light, their task would be impossible and begrudgingly agreed to return to the Eight Bells, and if Richard wasn't there, they would return at first light to continue their search. Crawford couldn't help but deduct a sense of guilt in his friend's behaviour.

Hill had seldom heard Crawford blaspheme, so on the rare occasion his friend did curse, he knew instinctively that something was wrong. Crawford was in severe pain; kneeling on all fours with his aged body hurting like hell, he stumbled over an obstacle which he assumed to be a discarded tree-trunk. He continued his swearing as Hill tried to get him to his feet. Hill thought the whole episode funny until he examined what his friend had tripped upon. It wasn't a discarded tree-trunk that had caused Crawford's agony – it was a dead body. The victim, as yet unknown, had been snared by a home-made deadly weapon. Both ankles had been severed from its legs by a heavy iron mantrap, causing severe blood loss, but that alone couldn't be the main cause of death.

They quickly identified the body as that of Richard Briggs; both fibulas had been severed in two, and judging by the considerable blood loss, he must have lain in absolute agony until his demise had been cruelly hastened by strangulation whilst he was calling for help, thereby returning the wood to peace and hush, save for the killer's silent footsteps.

Crawford visualised Briggs' death. He cried out in frustration as not being able to defend or help his colleague, he couldn't comprehend the sinful act. Crawford's pain was not just physical due to his recent stumble. He had to deal with the mental scares that would be permanently imprinted on his brain, just like at Waterloo when the seriously wounded were discarded along with the dead of all nations – English, Prussian, Dutch and French – without distinction and were stacked unceremoniously on top of each other in barns about the battlefield and set alight. The smell of burning flesh would remain forever inside his head alongside Robbie Burns' poem branded upon his heart,

'Many and sharp the num'rous ills
inwoven with our frame!
More pointed still we make ourselves
regret, remorse, and shame!
And man, whose heav'n-erected face
the smiles of love adorn, –
Man's inhumanity to man
makes countless thousands mourn!'

Hill was normally the steadier and stronger-minded person, but yet he was inconsolable in grief. He considered any assault on a friend to be an assault on himself, and Richard was his friend. Anger manifested inside Hill's body until he erupted; he punched the nearest tree without thinking of the harm he was causing himself; both men couldn't accept what had happened to their friend, their behaviour wouldn't be misplaced in a lunatic asylum. While Crawford took to silence, Hill acted as though he had been possessed by the devil himself.

It took some time before both men steadied themselves to process the predicament they had found themselves in. The very thought of continuing their journey through the dense undergrowth back to the Eight Bells in the darkness was foolish in the extreme. There was one important question that neither man had considered were there more traps ready and primed for Crawford and Hill to stumble upon? Were the traps the work of poachers or were they due to Lord Salisbury having problems with poachers? Whatever the answer, these killing machines had been deemed illegal ten years back. The possibility of being snared by a similar trap could bring fatal consequences or being maimed for life. The darkness that had wrapped the woods in his cosy blanket had blotted out the last remnants of twilight; the swaying of branches devoid of greenery except for the clinging ivy gave an impression of an impending gruesome conclusion.

Their priority was deciding whether to chance going back or stay where they were until daylight summoned the beginning of a new day. The logical choice suggested they should stay, but it was cold, and it had started to drizzle. Crawford posed the question and Hill considered his options, eventually agreeing to remain where they were, even if it meant huddled together, enduring a cold damp night in a Herefordshire wood. All things considered, it was agreed to put up with the discomforts of the wood than suffer an agonising death within the grips of a metal mantrap. 'Sleep well, David', Crawford jested with his friend, 'Piss off, John', he answered. With common sense prevailing, and despite the cold northerly wind combining with the drizzling rain, preventing either man from sleep, they remained safe on the woodland floor.

With the sun rising just after seven-thirty, both men returned worn-out, dirty and bedraggled to the warmth of the Eight Bells. Silas Kefford was shocked; he dropped the tea pot on the tavern floor, splattering its contents over his trousers and stockings. He hadn't realised his guests had been out all night; he presumed they were sleeping soundly in their beds.

'By God's mercy, what's happened?' he asked frantically.

CHAPTER 6

Watch and Observe!

Silas Kefford confirmed Richard Briggs hadn't slept in his room, and both Crawford and Hill had to, before going back into the woods, search for the missing colleague. 'I will make some strong tea with plenty of sugar; I hear that's good for shock'. Crawford thanked his host for his kind suggestion, but there would be plenty of time for rest and a hot soak after they had found their friend. His two guests were filthy after spending the night within the undergrowth of Hatfield's woodland; their clothes were ripped and soiled. Hill had an important question to ask before sipping his tea. He was enraged. As he snarled and ground his teeth together, his tone was of complete anger, and his body shook involuntary. He was about to speak, but he couldn't. His body was racked with pain, not for himself but for the friend he had been forced to abandon. It was never pleasant to witness a grown man cry. Lord Hill was in such a strong emotional state of grief that he was unable to continue. It was left to Crawford to ask the question.

'What my friend is trying to say is who left those evil mantraps scattered within Hatfield's woodland? Are they the work of poachers or land owners endeavouring to protect their livestock?'

Silas was shocked by the suggestion of any unlawful activities within his village. 'We ain't got poachers 'cause there ain't anything to poach, unless you think a few scrawny rabbits are fair game, and take it from me you don't need a bloody great big trap to snare a but a shotgun or slingshot is a far better way of keeping their numbers down'. Kefford turned away in disgust. 'What do you city dwellers know about the countryside, we have a trifling predicament with foxes, but they help reduce our cottontail population, and Salisbury's hounds used to keep the fox numbers down but since their retirement, Old Sally's hounds don't hunt in packs. They do, however, wander freely about the woods, and that is enough of a deterrent to convince Mister Fox to stay within his den'.

'So I can safely assume the traps were left for us'. Hill, without thinking, hissed back disapprovingly. His rage terrified Silas, who asked to be excused. 'Julia needs me in the kitchen'.

Crawford knew he had no alternative but to send another message back to Vickers to report on their predicament and to recall William Weaver back from France; he had no doubt Hatfield held the answer to the identity of the arsonist, but he also had to acknowledge that at present, neither man could leave the village with a killer at large. With the message written and sealed, he needed assurance that the message arrived safely. He contacted the local constable who agreed to deliver the note to Whitehall and wait for a reply. Three days later, the same constable returned to the Eight Bells with a sealed, confidential, letter addressed to Mister Crawford, who quickly opened the note and read its contents.

Trevaliant in Dover, Weaver has left France and on his way to England, Lizzie's whereabouts unknown, last seen four says ago at Downing Street.

Your humble servant Samuel Vickers.

Crawford read the note in complete silence; he hadn't seen much of Hill since they had brought Richard's body back from Hatfield wood. His remains had been secured inside the crypt of the local church, and that is where Hill had disappeared to every morning to have a one-sided conversation with a dead colleague.

Hill returned to the Eight Bells just before dusk, as was his usual custom since Richard's death. Crawford was sitting, deep in thought, by the bay-window towards the rear of the tavern. He casually waved to his friend as he walked into the Eight Bells, summoning him to join him. He ordered two whiskies from Hestia Kefford, who was on duty behind the bar. As Hill approached him, he felt the warmth of salty tears falling over his shallow cheeks, mingling into his beard. 'You look a mess', Hill said with real conviction, 'You look like shit yourself', Crawford replied. 'I have let everyone down, David', he sobbed, 'I didn't get the opportunity of getting to know Richard that well, but in the short time I knew him, he wasn't just a part of a team, he was a member of our special family', just as Crawford predicted and wanted them to become. Crawford moved about the room in a trance-like state, directionless as if lost within himself. Hill had rarely seen his friend look so emotionally drained as he aimlessly wandered within the confines of their rented accommodation. He picked up the letter from Vickers – not that any of its contents had altered – and put it down, before snatching it back again. Nothing had changed, no written word on the page had miraculously transformed into something more bearable. Hill had no idea how to bring his friend out of his disillusioned state, although he had heard a good slap on the face could assist in bringing someone back to reality when suffering from shock. He considered it but wondered if he would be doing more harm than good.

Hill shouted for help, but none came. 'Where is that idiot of a landlord!'

Suddenly Crawford spoke, as if waking up from a dream, 'Is Richard dead, or did I dream it?' Hill nodded confirming Crawford's question. Hill didn't know whether to respond or remain silent, 'What's the time and date?' Crawford asked. Hill responded by telling him it was just after five o'clock, Sunday the twenty-sixth of November. 'Why?'

'I'm expecting Lizzie tomorrow', he said, as his eyes squinted as if coming out from some hypnotic state. 'Listen to me, John. I'm the one who is considered unbalanced, what are you talking about, you read the message, Lizzie has gone assent without leave'. Hill was getting worried about Crawford's mental state, but decided to go along with his

105

conversation despite thinking that his friend was getting weirder and more unnerving by the minute. 'Yes, I have been in communication with Lizzie and she has confirmed she's on her way. We'll need her help when she arrives from London this time tomorrow. She might hold the key to unlock this horrid affair.' Having said that, Crawford downed his whisky in one gulp and moved towards the stairs and rest.

After the evening meal was cleared, Hill climbed the stairs to his room. He thought about knocking on Crawford's door to seek answers. Instead, he walked another ten yards to his own door, opened it and sat on the edge of his bed trying to make sense of today's activities. He sat alone, talking to himself, trying to make sense of what Crawford told him, but no one replied.

At precisely eight o'clock, Hill walked down the stairs to breakfast. Crawford was already seated, enjoying his first brew of the day. 'It will be good to see her again', Crawford offered polite conversation, 'Best look presentable before she arrives'. Hill had no idea what his friend was talking about. He thought, 'First he confesses to letting everyone down, then he starts talking gibberish and to cap it all he tells me Lizzie Drew, who has gone absent without leave is on her way here, the world's gone mad'.

John Crawford, the Samaritan, the leader of the pack, sat silently thinking how to respond to Hill's current dilemma, before quoting Edmund Burke, 'The only thing necessary for the triumph of evil is that good men do nothing. Do not allow evil to triumph, do not stand by and do nothing. David, you and I are the good men, this arsonist killer is pure evil, and he must not triumph over us'. That made perfect sense, perhaps the only sensible thing Crawford had of late told him.

Crawford took out his pocket watch from his fob pocket to check the time, telling Hill that Lizzie should arrive in less than thirty minutes unless any unforeseen difficulties had prolonged her journey. Lord Hill remained doubtful of Lizzie's arrival and strolled off in the direction of the church. He wanted to say a prayer over Richard's body, but being a non-believer, he didn't know any words for a suitable prayer. 'May I suggest a soldier's prayer? You were both soldiers. I trust you to come up with the right words', Crawford respectfully called out.

Hill thought long and hard about what to say over his fallen comrade, he didn't want it to sound wishy-washy but he needed it to sound compassionate, to have meaning, words that Richard himself might recite. But the words wouldn't come – he sat by the exit of the church, he didn't want to linger too long in case any of the locals thought him capable of stealing from the collection boxes,

A gentle tap on the shoulder brought him out of his torment. 'Forgive me, son', the vicar said, 'Can I help you in any way?' Reverend Boothby listened sympathetically to Hill's plight before going disappearing into his private office; he returned a few minutes later and offered Lord Hill a small card. 'This might help, my son', Boothby spoke with great tenderness and compassion. Hill read the card and looked about the church. For a while it was deserted; he was completely alone as he stood up and walked towards where the choir normally sat. St. Etheldreda's church was simply adorned; no fancy gold candle sticks or other gaudy symbols. Just one stained glass window with Etheldreda praying at Christ's crucifixion.

> *Dear Lord, I'm just a soldier,*
> *A protector of our land,*
> *A servant called to battle*
> *When my country takes a stand.*
> *I pray for strength and courage*
> *And a heart that will forgive,*
> *For peace and understanding*
> *In a world for all to live,*
> *My family's prayers are with me*
> *No matter where I roam,*
> *Please listen when I'm lonely,*
> *And return me safely home.*

Crawford was astonished at Hill's transformation as he re-entered the Eight Bells. He appeared to be full of piety. 'This won't last', Crawford thought to himself. 'I'm going upstairs for forty winks', Hill called out softly, 'Wake me if you need me'.

At four in the afternoon, Hill was woken from his brief sleep by fists banging on his bedroom door; it seemed only minutes had passed since he had trudged wearily upstairs to be wholly embraced by his soft warm bed-sheets. 'Alright', he shouted, 'I'm coming, keep your hair on'. He unlocked the bedroom door and peered into the corridor but saw no one. He heard Crawford gleefully shouting from downstairs, 'She's here! Get dressed'.

Hill cursed the inviting bed he so lovingly wanted to re-embrace as he hopped around the bedroom in an attempt to get his trousers on. Mission accomplished, he buttoned his shirt and opened the bedroom door, ready to go downstairs, before realising that in his sleepy posture, he had forgotten his socks and shoes. Eight minutes later, Hill walked downstairs to ascertain the cause of the recent commotion. He stopped dead in his tracks as his eyes focused on Lizzie Drew sipping tea with Crawford. It was Hill's turn to feel trapped in a hypnologic hallucination dream!

Lizzie shed a tear as she was told about Briggs' demise, until Hill banged his fist on the table, anxious to get his two penneth in, 'You can believe whatever you like, it wasn't an accident – Richard was murdered! What the hell is going on Lizzie, I thought you'd gone missing'.

Crawford knew his friend's recently found reverence wouldn't last too long; sure enough, he was back to his normal belligerent self. Lizzie tried to explain that she felt a compulsion to travel up to Hatfield, believing her friends were in desperate need of help. 'I'm not saying your arrival is unwelcome, far from it, but I don't understand any of this mumbo-jumbo that our friend has been going on about', Hill explained whilst pointing at Crawford. 'I just knew you were in trouble, it wasn't a premonition, it felt like an inner energy growing inside me. I certainly didn't know about Richard's death or the cause of it.

Anyway, whatever it was, and I can only describe it as a sense of knowing or being guided by an unseen friendly source, I am just as mystified as you are, but I can tell you one thing for certain – ever since I arrived at the Eight Bells, I have known evil resides inside this village.

'You know my thoughts concerning so-called mind readers and fortune-tellers: most are complete arseholes and money grabbing charlatans, but there are a few whom I acknowledge to be honourable men and women whom I admit appear to be plausible and give comfort, even when the church cannot. I have a talent for cold-reading which I proved before securing a place in the team'.

Hill was left open-mouthed; he still didn't fully understand Lizzie's explanation or her abilities to cold-read, but he was in full agreement with Lizzie when she told him evil was close-by – he had sensed that dread himself. Crawford was about to order three brandies when Lizzie put her gloved hand about his elbow. 'I feel something will happen this very night, and none of us has the power to prevent or stop it from happening. Whatever the evil deed is, it has already been recorded, and whatever fate has in store for us, we cannot alter'.

'Bloody hell Lizzie', Hill blurted out, 'I have goosebumps just thinking about what you've just said; surely we can't just sit and wait while murder is committed. There *must* be something we can do'. Lizzie calmly replied, 'Just watch and observe; see who leaves and see who enters. That's far more pertinent to me at this moment, for it is far too late to alter the course of fate. What is about to happen will happen, what has been written will transpire; we haven't the power to modify history. If we had more time, we might have been able to fine tune the future, whatever happens tonight will most certainly happen; if anyone is injured or worse, there is nothing we can do. Our sole objective is to watch and observe, and unlock any clues left behind, for I believe vital evidence will be displayed'.

Crawford looked pensive; he never really understood what went on inside Lizzie's head. He wondered if her gift was more of a curse than a blessing; Lizzie was his god-daughter, and he loved her dearly. However, he remained unclear on what he should be watching and where they should observe. Lizzie quickly answered, 'You will be right here, gentlemen'. 'Do you mean here inside the Eight Bells?' Hill interrupted the conversation.

'Yes', Lizzie softly replied.

Both men looked on, alarmed.

Lizzie calmly replied, 'Watch and observe'.

CHAPTER 7

Fire!

Crawford enquired what Lizzie would be doing whilst he and Hill were watching and observing. Her reply shocked both men as she answered, 'The wickedness in the beast is extremely heightened – I will stay within sight'. And that is exactly what she did, although both men were concerned over her well-being.

From five-thirty onwards, Silas and Julia Kefford were washing the table tops and repositioning chairs in readiness for the evening's trade. An elderly local man was busily bringing bottles of beer up from the cellars, while Hestia was upstairs changing bed clothes in the hope of attracting any additional customers who might be inclined to over drink and stay the night.

At six o'clock, everything was ready to accommodate the evening's trade, even though no one had left; but, more to the point, no one had entered. Lizzie's concerns were growing as she fidgeted in her chair; she couldn't sit any longer and casually stood up, wandering aimlessly about the tavern, moving from table to table under the watchful eye of Julia Kefford. She moved nonchalantly towards the Keffords, who remained behind the safe sanctuary of their bar. The potman was no more than one yard to the couples' right, making sure his display of bottles appeared tempting. Hestia remained upstairs, changing bed linen and sweeping the floors in the two rear rooms. Lizzie, noticing Silas, had moved away from his wife's side, changed her course and lingered awhile close to Julia. She hoped to make polite conversation with her in the hope of obtaining any mental images. If treachery existed within Julia Kefford, she couldn't perceive it, Lizzie was unable to penetrate her mind, either through her own tiredness – she had been travelling since early that morning – or had Julia been able to block Lizzie's attempts at breaching her mind, either way Lizzie withdrew and rejoined her male comrades at their table.

Lizzie sat and whispered to Crawford, 'Tell me a joke'. Crawford was amazed; he didn't know any jokes, jokes were not in his nature. 'I know one about a dog walking into a pub', he said, and started to tell his joke, but Crawford was right, he wasn't a natural joke teller; he had no timing as to when to deliver the punch line. It didn't matter as Lizzie, without warning, burst into laughter as if John Crawford had just told the greatest joke ever told. Lizzie kicked Hill in the legs in an attempt to get him laughing; she wanted to create an air of joy and pleasure; she was worried about the Keffords suspecting they were being secretly interrogated.

Silas Kefford sauntered from the bar and ambled towards the front door as if he was about to welcome his first customer of the evening, but no one was there. Noticing Kefford's departure, Lizzie swiftly ordered Crawford to stand beside their landlord and engage him in general chit-chat. Perhaps Lord Hill would have better luck talking to Julia

Kefford than she had. The potman made periodical appearances, bringing additional beer bottles up from the cellar and spread them evenly about the glassed shelving at the rear of the counter. Hestia stayed upstairs, as was indicated by the odd thumping noises from the upstairs bedrooms.

Crawford checked his pocket watch. Ten minutes past six, he thought to himself, before making sure his watch slid safely inside his waistcoat pocket. He hadn't given much thought about his chat with Silas. He started the conversation by talking about the weather; every Englishman loved to chat about the weather; sadly, Crawford found one that hadn't any interest in the November's weather; all he got from Silas were a couple of grunts. 'Did you ever serve in the army Mister Kefford?' That brought a favourable response from the landlord. 'I served at Waterloo and the peninsular campaign', he readily answered. 'I used to be a farrier, being a publican; all them damn horses required re-shoeing at least twice a month. I mainly worked with the officers; they were the ones with coin for tipping. The artillery gun-crews and cavalry troopers used to gamble or pissed their money away, not that I could blame them. Most of the officers were jumped up little boys who had only read about battles. I detested most of them rich dandies and what they stood for. I could never work out how we won battles with the useless shit Wellington had to contend with'. Crawford readily agreed he knew too many gentlemen who had paid for his son's commission, not like Bonaparte – he raised marshals and generals up from the ranks, even on the field of battle

.

114

Crawford couldn't disagree. He knew of bad officers who had suffered a bayonet in the back; he had even been tempted himself to contemplate such an act due to the Prince of Orange's stupidity at Waterloo. 'There were some good ones, Silas', Crawford asked. 'I remember a few. One good officer who came up from the ranks; Sharpe was 'is name, sharp by nature and Sharpe by name. No one could pull the wool over his eyes, 'e was a good officer, hallways 'ad time to chat with 'is men, hallways remembered a name'. 'And the shit ones?' Crawford asked, hoping Hill's name wasn't on Kefford's list.

'Well, Sir, I remained in France to oversee the peace and protect the locals from thieves and looters, but that didn't last too long. Soldiering costs money and after Waterloo, money was in short supply. Before Quatra-Bras, me and some of the lads were assigned under Hamerton's Essex boys; that is where I first cast me eyes on the biggest load of shit in the British harmy, has I 'ave already told you 'alf the hofficers we had to contend with were rubbish, but a few stick out 'ead and shoulders 'bove the worst. They were the bully boys, the drunkards and womanisers. The shit on top of my list was a vicar's son from this very county, Captain Edward Boyd was 'is name, 'e caused many a hargument between us in the ranks and took great pleasure in upsetting the locals. It was Boyd's gang of shits that stole food from the villagers and it was 'im and his bullies who raped the women and young girls. The Provost Marshal's nearly caught him once, but they hung the wrong man – they hung an innocent lad from hereabouts, no more than fifteen 'e was'.

'Boyd was a right old bastard, 'e finally got 'is just desserts at Quatra-Bras. Ney's army of the north should 'ave beaten us up and spit us out, but as you know, we regrouped and joined up with Nosey just south of Waterloo'.

'What happened to Captain Boyd?' Crawford asked.

'It was when Prince Jérôme's Frenchie's pushed us out from the Bossu Wood. The Captain was under the command of General John Millett Hamerton of the East Essex Regiment, the 44th Foot Regiment. Lovely man, that Hamerton, but Boyd was an absolute shit, run away so 'e did, and in doing so, the coward got 'is just rewards when two Polish Lancers caught up with the bastard and found the spineless lump of dog-turd did 'ave a spine after all. The lads found 'im and left 'im where 'e fell. They took some souvenirs from 'im, so we did, and that's 'ow I managed to buy this place'.

'Thank you, Silas', Crawford endeavoured to rejoin his friends, but Silas was in full flow, anxious to tell his story. 'From that day onwards, Julia came back to England with me, we married at the local church here in Hatfield soon after our return. I 'ad to give up soldiering as Julia was always worried if I would be coming back or if I lay dead in some foreign field. She's a good woman, she might be a good few years my junior, but she always stuck with me, through thick and thin, God only knows why. Never thought I would be a father, but eight months after our wedding, Hestia was prematurely born 'ere at the Eight Bells, God bless 'er'.

While Crawford was talking with Silas Kefford, Lizzie suggested that Hill should try to engage in conversation with Julia. Perhaps he would have better luck than she. At first, Julia appeared anxious, especially when her husband had briefly stepped outside with John Crawford; she cleverly changed the course of the chat, much to Hill's annoyance by running her husband down. Her only concern seemed to be for her daughter. 'She must be a big help to you, being a publican is not as easy as it looks'. Hill tried to regain the initiative by praising Hestia. Hill recognised a natural bond between mother and daughter. He detected a slight degree of repugnance towards her husband, as if she wanted him to be more assertive, but she didn't expand on what she wanted him to be aggressive about. Hill had the feeling that Julia Kefford was the dominant partner in the marriage, and Silas was nothing more than a lackey. Whether he had always been a pawn in this clear marriage of convenience Hill could not tell, and as he had yet had no chance to speak to Hestia, he could see where she fitted into the equation. The conversation abruptly ended when a high-pitched noise from the kitchen signified a kettle was about to boil. Hill thanked Misses Kefford for her time as the two parted in different directions, Julia to the kitchen and Hill to a table where Lizzie Drew was waiting patiently to hear his initial impressions of a woman possibly scorned. Hill sat alongside Lizzie to impart his impressions of the landlady; he repeated the conversation word for word as near as possible, trying not to leave anything out. Lizzie lifted her eyebrows in surprise when Hill mentioned the word 'bond', 'Are you sure that is what she said, or implied? It just seems an unusual term when talking about mother and

117

daughter'. Hill turned to look questioningly at Lizzie, 'What term would you use?', he asked. 'Did the word love ever pop up in the conversation?', Lizzie queried. 'No, strange that, don't you think, but then I have never sired a daughter, only a son, and men don't talk about love in the way that women do'. Crawford returned to a few minutes after Hill and sat somewhat despondently between Hill and Lizzie. 'I lay short odds that Silas is much henpecked. He clearly adores his daughter and worships the ground she walks on; he undoubtedly enjoys reminiscing about his army days, but he never once showed any feelings towards his wife. It's as if she just come into his life like a new chapter in a book'.

From the constant sound of beds scratching along the floors upstairs, Hestia was still busily cleaning the final two unoccupied bedrooms. Crawford heard a door being forcibly closed and locked, followed by a second door closing less than thirty seconds later. Hestia had finished her duties for the day as she skipped downstairs and hurried into the kitchen for her meal. Hestia was a pretty young girl; it was obvious she took after her mother; she had inherited her exquisite facial looks and beautiful eyes from Julia, whilst Lizzie could see any resemblance towards her father. Silas had a round piggy nose and bulging eyes that might frighten young babies whereupon their mothers would find it had to pacify them.

Silas Kefford had evidently smoked his clay pipe, a habit he kept from his wife. He waved his hand in front of his mouth to clear away any lingering tobacco smell, but Julia had already guessed the real reason why her husband had returned a few minutes after Crawford. The look of sheer repugnance on his wife's face gave it away. Silas lowered his head in total submission as he sauntered back to the bar counter. As he rejoined his wife, Julia gave a look of revulsion before swiftly disappearing into the kitchen. No doubt Silas would pay later for his apparent lapse of abstinence. Hill whispered, 'Easy to see who wears the trousers in this household'.

Crawford shouted to Silas, 'Business is unnaturally slack today, Mister Kefford'. He was forced to raise his voice due to the commotion outside. Kefford walked back to his three guests to explain, 'I hear more guests have arrived at Hatfield House; most of my customers will be busy conveying those additional guests up to the house by using their pony and traps – it will be busier soon, don't you worry'.

It was close to six-forty when old Tom and his mongrel entered the bar. They strolled up to the bar where Silas had a half-pint of ale waiting his arrival. Old Tom moved away from the bar to a table and single chair, evidently his reserved space within the Eight Bells. Less than five minutes had passed when six or seven frantic farmers rushed into the tavern, exclaiming the big house to be on fire. 'The chapel has already been lost, and the rest of the west wing is burning out of control'.

Lizzie looked at her two colleagues in alarm. 'No one has left, and only old Tom and his flea-bitten dog had entered'. Tom was a regular at the Eight Bells and normally arrived later, but tonight, probably due to the party at the big house, he had decided to come earlier to purchase his customary one and a half pints to enjoy his drink in relative peace and quiet.

Lizzie suggested her friends quickly join her outside; she required privacy. She knew something would happen and instinctively knew it would involve the arsonist, but her gamble in thinking that the Keffords were in some way implicated appeared incorrect; they had been under their observation throughout the afternoon. 'Surely, Old Tom can't be our arsonist. He looks more like a crippled scarecrow than a fire raiser', Lizzie explained. Lord Hill half-smiled and said, 'Well, if it ain't old Tom, my money's on the dog'. Lizzie shot a look of contempt at Hill, 'You are out of order', she cried. She knew from her dream that Crawford needed help; she also knew a fire would be started tonight. She had picked up on that too – but she had missed something.

The old potman looked startled, wondering if he should help with the fire at the big house. Silas and Hestia Kefford both looked traumatised in disbelief that evil had come to visit their community. Lizzie called out to Crawford, Hill, Silas and the old potman. 'Move your arses or else the fire will likely spread to take away your livelihoods'. Silas hadn't thought about the fire spreading to his little public house to consume his source of revenue. He didn't need telling twice as the four men dashed up towards the blaze at Hatfield House,

Everyone, with the exception of the three women, had raced up to the big house to assist in extinguishing the blaze. When the villagers arrived at

120

the scene, the entire west wing was ablaze. The site was one of total chaos, the locals were running around like headless chickens, busily doing nothing. To prevent the fire from spreading to the rest of the house, the villagers set about stripping the countless number of tapestries, books, artwork and furniture and storing them in a place of safety within the surrounding parkland under the stewardship of the local yeomanry.

Fire crews from Barnet were first on the scene, but they found themselves ineffectual due to the lack of water pressure. Her Ladyship and Captain Grimston had evacuated every child from inside the house and put them into a place of safety. Initially, it was agreed that everyone was safe and accounted for; however, it soon became evident that the Dowager Marchioness was missing. Her maid and a man servant had confirmed to Lord Salisbury that his mother had been last witnessed retiring to her room ten minutes before the outbreak of fire. With scant regard to their own safety, His Lordship and his servant valiantly tried to reach the Dowager's suite; however, due to the extreme heat, combined with smouldering timbers creating thick black smoke engulfing the interior of the building, both men were forced back from their futile attempt at rescue. Everyone had to consider their own safety; it became apparent from the imminent threat of floors and ceilings collapsing, as well as the increased heat generating from within the heart of the blaze, that all was lost. They had to leave it to the fire crew and their bravery.

The firemen were obstructed from carrying out their duties due to the thickness of the stone wall that lay between the chapel and the rest of the west wing. A large fire engine was dispatched from the County Fire Office and arrived on the scene just after ten in the evening, by which time the lead on the old roof had melted and with it most of the west wing. There was total confusion, especially when the hefty reservoir on top of the house burst, allowing gallons of water to flood the lower floors. Smouldering timbers, mud and thick muddy ash and singed fabrics brought the terrifying site into focus. With the firemen slowly gaining control over the fire, thanks principally to the water from the huge reservoir quenching the fire's thirst, at least three-quarters of Hatfield House had been saved. Lord Salisbury and his family were inconsolable when it was confirmed that the Dowager had perished within the building. She had been the sole fatality of the fire.

It was not deemed safe to enter the building until the second day after the fire had been brought under control, and then only with the guidance of the fire crew who remained on site as a precaution. What remained of the Dowager's body had been recovered from her suite; however, her collection of fine jewellery, including a beautiful necklace presented to the Cecil family by King Charles II of Scotland and an extraordinary pearl necklace presented to the celebrated Countess of Salisbury by King Edward II, together with countless other rare diamonds said to be of immense value, had vanished, presumed to have been destroyed as a result of the fire.

On the afternoon following the fire, Crawford and Hill reported in person to the Prime Minister, Lizzie stayed at Hatfield, still having deep suspicions regarding the Kefford family, but her talents for cold-reading and her newly acquired sixth-sense remained dormant. She had always vehemently maintained she wasn't a clairvoyant or fortune-teller; the vast majority of those who called themselves that were in her view charlatans and swindlers, preying on the vulnerable. Lizzie had practiced cold-reading techniques over the years; she considered herself to be a good one. 'All I need is more time with the Keffords to lift their veil of concealment and draw it asunder', she thought.

Lizzie wondered if her doubts, that were related to her experiences when she was called to Crawford's side, had in some way traumatised her brain, thereby causing the ninety odd percent of the brain that we don't use to temporarily switch off and reject out of hand the acceptance of what at the time seemed so real, but now seemed so illusory.

Rumours surrounding the fire and the Dowager's death were rife. Gossip was spreading that the fire had been deliberately started to conceal a robbery, while others openly said someone held a grudge against the Salisbury family – all complete rubbish of course!

To silence the rumours, the Prime Minister, Viscount Melbourne, prepared a carefully worded statement confirming that the death of the Dowager was nothing more than a terrible accident, the cause of which appeared to be the dropping of a lit candle.

Neither Crawford nor Hill could refute or prove otherwise. If any proof existed, the fire had consumed every trace. Crawford tried in vain to express his suspicions and, as far as the agency was concerned, the case remained open.

Melbourne was getting weary of empty promises – he urgently wanted a result. Regular retractions appertaining to arson attacks made him look inadequate and stupid. The Prime Minister couldn't afford to look either. If any arrests were made in the future by Crawford or his team, they wouldn't be able to associate it with the recent fires at Westminster or Hatfield.

William Lamb
(Viscount Melbourne)
Prime Minster of Great Britain 1835–1841

CHAPTER 8

St. Etheldreda's Church

Lizzie was convinced the Kefford's were involved in some way with the recent events; her only problem was she couldn't fathom out which one it might be, or whether all of them were implicated. Crawford and Hill, along with Lizzie, had carefully observed the family's movement during the afternoon of the fire and none of them had left the Eight Bells. Lizzie recalled Crawford's conversation with Silas Kefford in relationship to his army career. Apart from his loathing of an Edward Boyd, the vicar's son from hereabouts, he looked upon the army as his extended family.

With very little to occupy her mind whilst her colleagues were in London, she opted to stroll around the village. The parish of Hatfield was extremely pretty, even in winter. The neighbourhood was primarily a combination of rich arable land, permanent grassland for livestock to graze upon and sufficient woodland to reduce any problems with soil erosion. From what she knew about the village, it was plainly evident the region was originally a forest, on which the Salisbury estate appeared most prominent. The greater part of the parish appeared hilly, especially towards the north around the hamlets of Handside and Brocket Park. Looking south-east, the ground rose considerably, especially near Woodhill.

The River Lea, a tributary of the Thames, flowed through the parish, entering at Brocket Park before diagonally crossing east to west before exiting through the northern most location of Home Park which created a natural boundary near the little village of Holwell. Lizzie was aware that the mail coach used the Great North Road that ran through the heart of the parish, crossing the main road through Saint Albans and Hertford. With all the hullabaloo of recent days, Lizzie was in need of peace and quiet, and what better place to find both attributes than the local church? The old stone church stood just west of the centre of the village on top of a slight incline. The main door was open, and the sound of complete silence made it instantly clear to Lizzie that she was totally alone in the church. She wandered idly through its cold uninviting interior; she passed a small table with various leaflets and parish notices scattered over its surface, one of which explained to any curious visitors the history of the church and the reasoning behind its name. Etheldreda was an Anglo-Saxon saint; apparently the name had greater significance in nearby Ely. Etheldreda or Audrey had been an East Anglian Princess from the Fenland, as well as the Abbess of Ely and a Queen of Northumbria. Lizzie casually replaced the leaflet on the table before picking up another leaflet concerning the historical background of Hatfield House. It seemed the residents could trace the records of the house back to the time of the Bishops of Ely. During its long history it had been a welcoming playground for royal visitors, including Elizabeth Tudor, the daughter of Henry VIII and Anne Boleyn. The present owner, the second Marquess of Salisbury, James Brownlow William, had followed in his father's footsteps by becoming

Member of Parliament of the constituency of Weymouth in Dorset, and subsequently he asked to be considered as a commissioner on Indian affairs.

Lizzie thought she understood the connection between the Bishops of Ely and an East Anglian Princess who died more than two thousand years ago. Her eyes casually glanced over the various leaflets and parish notices mainly connected with banns of forthcoming marriages; everything looked in perfect order, neatly piled together by an overly tidy churchwarden, when without warning one leaflet seemed to fly effortlessly from the table on to the stone floor. She checked if she had closed the door before entering the church – yes, it was shut, no sudden breeze could be the cause, but the pamphlet was on the floor. She considered leaving the note on the floor; after all, she wasn't to blame for its disturbance, but she bent down to pick up the offending handbill, not intending to read the escaping leaflet. She checked for similar notes on the table and soon found its siblings. Lizzie placed the brochure on top of the pile when her attention was drawn to the bold-type – the leaflet provided information for any visitor regarding previous organists, choir masters, churchwardens and vicars who had served the parish and church of St. Etheldreda. To Lizzie's amazement, one name appeared to stand out from the rest – William Edward Boyd had been the vicar of this church between 1799 and 1818. Lizzie wondered if the Boyds still resided in the village or even in one of the nearby hamlets. She replaced the brochure and left the church with as much respect and reverence as she could muster. Lizzie's brain went into overdrive; she quickly began combining facts in an attempt to bring

127

credence and verification to previously unrelated pieces of information, one of which she hoped to substantiate herself by connecting Captain Edward Boyd with the Reverend William Edward Boyd. How did a vicar's son from Herefordshire, a gambler, womaniser and a bully, an officer in Wellington's victorious army, lose his life in consequence of his cowardice by turning his back to run from the French at Quatra-Bras?

She wondered if the Boyd family still resided in the village of Hatfield or in any of the nearby villages. A faint glimmer of a smile beamed across her pale face as she walked from the church; she felt self-conscious that her actions might be construed as anything other than a curious visitor seeking historical facts regarding the picturesque village of Hatfield and its environs. As she slowly made her way out of the church grounds, she became aware of another presence close-by. From the corner of her eye, she noticed a shadowy figure walking around the back of the church's tower. Lizzie had always been inquisitive and decided to amass every ounce of her inner energy to repel any negative forces that might wish to inflict harm on her. Lizzie felt the enormous feeling of relief swiftly subsiding from her body when she twisted about and accidently collided with the Reverend Boothby. They both promptly introduced themselves to each other and before long, Lizzie asked the burning question she urgently needed to clarify: the relationship, if any, between Captain Edward Boyd and the Reverend William Edward Boyd.

Boothby confirmed they were father and son. Captain Boyd had been killed fighting the French a few days prior to the great battle at Waterloo; meanwhile his father had prayed for the souls of the dead killed in action at Waterloo and all those conflicts that had faded into history, even though they remained carved into the souls of their loved ones, which included his one and only son. 'Can I speak to the Reverend Boyd?' she asked. Boothby explained that 'the reverend died at the vicarage as a result of a serious fire, probably caused by a spark from his fire jumping onto his rug. The vicarage quickly caught fire and within thirty minutes the place had been reduced to ash'.

Although Lizzie's heart pounded in her slim torso, her head joyfully spun as she took in every piece of information. She realised, beyond a shadow of doubt, that there was proof, albeit circumstantial, connecting the Kefford and Boyd families. In addition, she thought she recognised a political link between the Salisbury family and the Houses of Parliament, cumulating in the resignation of Lord Grey. Everything made sense in Lizzie's mind, but why revert to murder and discrediting? What could possibly be the motive for at least one member of the Kefford family to feel the urge, or uncontrollable desire, to start fires that could end in killing innocent individuals? She had a lot to think about on her way back to the Eight Bells.

As she returned to her lodgings, she felt uncomfortable. Silas Kefford was as usual standing behind the bar, and he enquired if she had enjoyed her ramble through Hatfield. Lizzie smiled an agreeing nod of the head as she climbed the stairs to her bedroom. She would feel safer when Crawford and

Hill returned, but that wouldn't be until tomorrow. Until then, she had to make the best of a bad situation.

As she lay on her bed, she thought about everyone who had died – the reverend, his son, Richard Briggs and now the Dowager Marchioness, the first Lady Salisbury, but there might be others. Lizzie held on to the belief – her one small piece of comfort, her ability and talent to cold-read; she had been distracted from her gift due to recent events, but she believed her flair for appearing to read the thoughts and minds of others could be encouraged and enhanced. She felt confusion and perplexity within herself, she asked herself, 'What caused the leaflet in the church to suddenly flutter to the floor? There was no draft or breeze to assist its descent'. She had no way of controlling inanimate objects; however, it was an indisputable fact that one minute, the leaflet was on the table, and the next it was lying face up on the cold floor, as if some invisible force had played out the occurrence. If she thought about the strange phenomenon for too long, she would surely go doolally. She had entertained guests at dinner parties with her powers of misdirection and persuasion; she wasn't a mystic or fortune-teller, and she certainly wasn't someone who held a belief that all objects and knowledge, including the physical universe, ultimately had no existence except as creations of the mind.

Lizzie's brain was spinning inside her head. She seemed to be questioning herself, and, what was worse, her brain was answering back. 'What am I talking about? I am bamboozling myself in talking mumbo jumbo'. She felt a tremendous pounding inside her skull; her head spun as if suffering from a bad hangover, but at the same time she felt like she was paralysed. Being wholly incapable of movement, all her preconceived judgements bounced off one another, as if some as yet unknown, concealed, influence had taken control over her body and lifted it up to a superior plane. She looked down upon her own body as it lay lifeless on the bed below. Everything she was experiencing should have been in direct contradiction to her beliefs, but her shift in perspective regarding a supernatural phenomenon were alien to her. She hadn't experienced anything like this before. Bizarre and intriguing thoughts came flooding into her mind, filling the void with plenty of questions but offering little in the way of answers. The name 'Kefford' kept stabbing at her intelligence and simultaneously warning her to be ultra-careful.

She remained powerless to move as she lay on her bed. She tried to blink her eyes to no avail; she could see and hear but couldn't stir her body into action. She could hear Kefford arguing with his wife downstairs, but the words were muffled and meaningless. She felt a sudden urge to jump off the bed when the doorknob rattled and turned. 'Who is it?' she timidly enquired. But no one replied. Her brief paralysis had left her. At last, she had the power of movement. Lizzie swiftly ran to the door, but no one was there. She looked along the half-lit hallway, but no one was there. Had she imagined her last ten minutes? She hadn't been dreaming, she told herself, she could still hear the Keffords arguing downstairs. Nevertheless, something had startled her into full consciousness. Lizzie had two choices – to stay where she was or venture downstairs. Her heart told her to stay put, but her brain ordered her to go downstairs. Lizzie became aware of something trying to communicate with her. They weren't voices as she knew them, they were more of a sense of knowing she afterwards related to. Whatever she thought she was listening to, the sounds appeared to be distressed by their failure to communicate with her.

If this was part of a new-found talent, she didn't want any part of it. Unable to comprehend her surroundings, she screamed. Until she was able to control this gift, she wanted to be left in peace and quiet, but the feelings grew more intense, filling her head to the point of bursting. Lizzie cried out, but not in pain or sorrow; she wasn't sure about her feelings anymore.

Lizzie was confused and so were the Keffords when they found her lying prostrate on the floor of the tavern. She had fainted.

When she regained consciousness, she found Crawford sitting beside her on the bed. She tried in vain to sit up, but her body was too weak to support her weight. 'Let me help you', Crawford volunteered, 'we have all been terribly worried about your health. Can you explain what happened?'

Lizzie tried to explain, but how can you explain the unexplainable? She started by trying to describe the uncanny way her senses of knowing grew steadily louder within her. She knew she wasn't making any sense, and she knew it by the way Crawford screwed his face in disbelief and scepticism. She tried to reassure Crawford by telling him not to

132

worry; she had only fainted and would be back to her usual self after resting. 'When did you faint?' Crawford asked. Lizzie looked suspiciously and carefully at Crawford, before answering his question. 'Last night just before the evening meal. Why do you ask?'

Crawford rubbed his chin; he also needed time to formulate his reasons for asking. 'According to the doctor, you have been unconscious for nearly four days. When David and I returned from London, he informed us you hadn't suffered a fracture of the skull as there were no signs of bruising or cuts. He assumed you suffered a black-out. Do you remember anything apart from what you have already recalled?'

'Four days...' Lizzie replied, unable to comprehend his answer, 'Who undressed me, put me to bed, cared for my needs and put my nightgown on?'

'You have Hestia Kefford to thank for all of that', he replied. 'Apparently she has been fussing over you like a mother hen ever since your accident'.

Lizzie couldn't understand; how could her prime suspect be willing to help her?

Crawford suggested that once she felt stronger, all three of them should take some fresh air and take the opportunity of walking about the village. 'I have much to tell you, dear', he told her. 'I have much to tell you', she impatiently replied as she tried to get the bedclothes from her body. 'Let's wait until this afternoon, or at least until you dress yourself", he grinned.

CHAPTER 9

Court Marshal

By three in the afternoon, Lizzie had rested enough. With Hestia's help, she dressed and met with Crawford and Hill downstairs. She looked pale and thinner following her ordeal; her makeup had concealed the redness in her eyes and with the help of a splatter of rouge about her checks, she looked reasonably well. The trio needed privacy to talk freely, away from unwanted, prying ears. Although the weather was overcast, a slight northerly breeze brought the temperature down, but at least the drizzle which plagued most of southern England had dissipated. Lizzie informed her companions about what she had learnt from Reverend Boothby about to the demise of the Reverend William Edward Boyd in a fire at the vicarage ten years ago. Lizzie considered this to be the focal point of the arsonist's anger and everything that followed – the pressure put on Earl Grey to resign his position as Prime Minister, the fire at the Houses of Parliament in '35 and finally the fire at Hatfield House which resulted in the unintentional deaths of Lady Salisbury and poor Richard Briggs. Maybe Richard was killed because they were getting too close to identifying the arsonist, or arsonists. 'You think there might be more than one, Lizzie?' Crawford enquired. 'I do, sir', she replied. 'And besides your impressions that the coded messages might have had two authors, what else gives you that idea?' Crawford continued.

Crawford suggested Lizzie remain quiet while Hill explained what information he had gathered from Horse Guards. 'And don't interrupt until you have heard everything'.

'Whilst you surmise that the Reverend Boyd was murdered in his vicarage in the summer of 1827, we think the focal point goes back much further, probably as far back as June 1815'.

'According to the classified military records written-up a couple of days prior to the skirmish at Quatra-Bras, General Hamerton had been ordered by His Grace the Duke of Wellington to either prove or refute allegation of gross indecency, theft, rape and murder against Captain Edward Boyd, together with a few others under the Captain's command. The Provost Marshal's arrested Boyd and securely held him in a small outhouse in the village of Sombreffe, just east of Quatra-Bras. Witnesses were called, all of whom to a man testified against Boyd, confirming they had witnessed him stealing money and food from the villagers and generally terrorising the locals into submission with threats of severe beatings. His vilest crimes were charges of multiple rapes, with some of his victims being only in their early teens'. Hill paused for breath allowing Lizzie to comprehend all that she was being told

'The case Hill and I were particularly interested in concerned a young girl aged about fifteen; she was raped in front of her parents.

Subsequently, the entire population of the village, a total of thirty or so individuals – men, women and children, the elderly and babies – were incarcerated within their small church and the building set alight. Due to the bravery of a few English redcoats, they managed to save the lives of two people, the young girl and her uncle. The rest, including her parents, all died a horrible death'.

The court marshal found Boyd guilty, with a unanimously verdict and sentenced him to be executed by firing squad the following morning. But unfortunately, Marshall Ney's French force arrived on the scene earlier than anticipated, thereby offering Boyd a temporary escape from his fate'.

Lizzie was about to talk, but Crawford curtly told her to be quiet. 'Remember what I said, no interruptions until you have heard all Hill has to say'.

'I agree with what you might say Lizzie, but listen carefully', Crawford reminded his god-daughter, as Hill continued with his report, 'If we consider the focal point of the atrocities to be June 1815 and not the summer of 1827, we must conclude that the Keffords cannot conceivably be responsible as perpetrators of the crimes'.

'What about revenge as a motive?' Lizzie shouted to Hill. Crawford turned to glance at Lizzie, 'Be quiet, girl!' he shouted back as some of the locals began noticing a quarrel developing within their unassuming little village.

'Let Hill finish', he said, trying to keep a lid on the argument. Crawford glared at Lizzie, as if beating her into submission, as Hill once again tried to complete his intelligence report. 'There is one massive hole in your summary of Silas Keffords involvement. First, private Kefford had been assigned to protect Hamerton's vanguard when Boyd was killed, and secondly, I can categorically tell you that according to Hamerton's own roll-call, Kefford was at Waterloo on the morning of Boyd's death. Boyd wasn't killed by Polish lancers or by English redcoats; his naked body was found tied to a tree in the centre of Sombreffe, with his throat cut, possibly the result of Frenchmen taking their own revenge against Englishmen'.

'The Provost Marshal's Office testified that Captain Boyd was likely killed on the morning of the sixteenth day of June 1815, at which time private Kefford was busily retreating with Hamerton's force from the crossroads of Quatra-Bras to join up with Wellington's main force at La Haye Sainte. We have over thirty witnesses confirming his alibi'.

Crawford apologised to Lizzie for his rudeness in keeping her quiet. 'It is impossible for Silas Kefford to be the murderer of Captain Boyd. The local authorities considered Boyd's death to be committed by local villagers, but as there were no witnesses, nothing could be proved'.

Lizzie looked thoroughly dejected. She had thought she had solved the case single-handedly, but if Kefford was innocent and the parents of the girl had perished in the pursuing inferno, the only one left was a fifteen-year-old girl. 'For God's sake, Lizzie, be quiet!' Hill was determined to have the last word on the matter, 'You will learn more by listening than continually interrupting!'

Crawford once again asked Hill to complete his report. 'I found out the name of that fifteen-year-old girl. It had been filed away in the Marshal's documentation records. Her full name was Juliette Noureddine, the only child of Louisa and Jacque Noureddine. Louisa was an English school teacher working in Belgium'.

'That doesn't tell us too much', Lizzie sombrely replied, glancing at Crawford as if asking if she could speak. 'O but it does Lizzie, it's not that much of a leap of faith to connect Juliette with Julia. If Juliette was fifteen when raped, she would be thirty-seven now, and how old do you think Mrs. Kefford is now?'

Lizzie quickly understood where Hill was taking her, and for the first time since the three of them began their stroll about the village, Lizzie was speechless.

Understanding Lizzie's lack of comments, John Crawford added a single word – 'Exactly'.

Lizzie regained her composure by purposely throwing a huge spanner in the works. 'Julia couldn't be our arsonist; she was in full view of all the three of us throughout the afternoon prior to the fire at Hatfield House, cleaning the bar with Silas by her side. She didn't leave the Eight Bells'.

Crawford glanced skyward, towards the heavens. 'Sod it, I hadn't considered that!'

'Back to square one', Lizzie agreed.

'Not really, Lizzie', Hill declared. 'We have circumstantial evidence connecting the Kefford family to the murders and arson attacks. We just don't have proof; what we have to do is re-evaluate and decipher what we *think* we know with what we *do* know and try to make sense of it all. The motive holds water; our only problem is that we cannot place any of our suspects at the scene of the crimes'.

Crawford and Lizzie Drew reluctantly agreed with Lord Hill, and both concluded that a complete restart with the investigation wouldn't go amiss; initially, they should delve deeper into the killing of Captain Boyd. 'May I respectfully suggest the recall of Samuel Vickers from France? I think we all agree that the Prime Minister's aides are innocent of any involvement'.

'What we know and can prove', Lizzie continued, 'is that Silas Kefford was not in Sombreffe when Boyd was killed. We know that Silas and Julia or Juliette Kefford, thanks to us, have an cast-iron alibi to make them incapable of being responsible for the fire at Hatfield House; that only leaves Hestia'. Crawford was astonished, 'She was upstairs all afternoon'. 'Did you see her?' Lizzie wanted to know. 'Well, no', Crawford answered, 'but we all heard her'. 'Hearing is not seeing, Mister Crawford', Lizzie concluded her cross examination. Was there any possibility that Hestia might have been instructing someone to act on her behalf to assist in committing such a heinous crime?

'Too many ifs and buts for my liking', Hill concluded. 'Whatever happened at Sombreffe needs to be explored in greater detail. It resonated in horrific crimes and terminated in the killing of Captain Boyd. The unsolved mystery of the Reverend Boyd's death in the vicarage needs further investigation; it is far too easy to explain it away as just being accidental in nature. Next in our chain of events come the coded messages written in French and sent to Earl Grey. If you recall, Louisa was an English school teacher married to a Belgian where we have a multitude of dialects, including French, Dutch, Flemish and German, so it not unreasonable to assume Louisa passed on her language skills to her daughter. 'I've not heard Misses Kefford speak in any other language than English', Crawford butted in. 'And you're forgetting Julia Kefford has us as reliable witnesses to proclaim her innocence'.

'What about the slaying of Richard?' Lizzie asked. 'Silas Kefford has you as a witness', she respectfully imparted to Crawford.

Hill admitted defeat; they were just going around in circles. They had spent the last hour speculating without coming up with anything that might point to the arsonist, but Hill being Hill, he was determined to have the last word. 'Think on this, what if every member of the Kefford family could be implicated, father, mother and daughter – is that beyond the realms of possibility?'

141

Both Lizzie and Crawford considered the possibility and couldn't disagree with Hill's logic, which might be the only credible answer to the crimes, but Lizzie wasn't satisfied. She had serious misgivings but kept them to herself.

95th Riffle Brigade at Waterloo

CHAPTER 10

Memento Mori
(Remember you too must die)

Unlike Crawford and Hill, Lizzie had a restless night; her fears clashed with her misgivings to merge head-on in an attempt to protect her from any unseen dangers. She had always considered her mind-reading performances to be nothing more than an innocent parlour trick, but now she felt violated. Something was trying to influence and control her. In the past, Lizzie had experienced bizarre and strange emotions by predicting beforehand what people would say before saying it – a type of foreknowledge.

In her dream, she had sensed Crawford was in danger. She instinctively knew it was her duty to help the man – it was a premonition, or a sense of knowing that demanded her presence back at Hatfield. She knew animals had a far greater sense of awareness than humans, which allowed them to predict dangers, principally in forecasting thunder storms. As a young girl, her family always had pets in the house – dogs mainly. She knew their sense organs allowed them to predict changes in the environment; she was also aware that some animals could sense changes in magnetic fields. These sense organs stimulated the animals' sixth-sense by producing nerve impulses that travelled to the brain via an ultra-sensory nerve; perhaps this self-same sixth-sense had developed within her. She certainly had a greater awareness of magnetic and electrical fields. She knew her feelings or senses at present were silent, although she knew something was guiding her, and whatever that something was, it had no relationship with evil – of that she was sure. She didn't feel any immediate harm threatening her. She didn't feel anxious, but she did feel different.

She peered out of the window to watch the sun rise; she was hesitant to face the new dawn. Lizzie had judged it to be around six in the morning. She could relax for another hour before breakfast was served. The cockerel had yet to announce the heralding of a new day, but as sure as eggs were eggs, his habitual song would soon wake the entire village.

Lizzie fidgeted slightly in her bed; she embraced the warmth of the sheets as they curled around her body. Her senses became heightened as she perceived a shadow drift passed her window; she was no longer afraid, although she did notice a strange message written by a finger on her window. She had always been confident in her self-preservation, but now in the half-light of morning she no longer felt apprehensive or fearful. She was ready for whatever the fresh day would bring. All her fears had left her; she felt an inward strength growing from within, and whatever the day had on offer, she would be positive.

The cockerel commenced its morning screech, and Lizzie slid her feet on to the cold floor. It was time to wash, dress and follow whatever her spirit guide demanded of her. If she had any remaining doubts, they had vanished. She was ready to confront her enemies and embrace her unique beneficence. Her inner energy and strength no longer demanded anything from her. From this day forward, she felt content to let her guide show her the way.

She realised for the first time in her life that her days of entertaining friends with her parlour tricks were over. She now had a wondrous competence deep inside her and craved to utilise it solely for goodness. She couldn't become a fraudster swindling the bereaved out of their last penny; she had a much higher opinion of herself than to delve amongst the insipid. Feeling an internal light shining throughout her body, she walked downstairs.

'By God, Lizzie, you look ravenous this morning! Thought you might have problems sleeping last night', Hill asked in his usual haughty manner.

Lizzie didn't bother to reply. She just needed a pot of tea to quench her thirst and shake off the miseries of the previous sleepless nights. Once that first drink was inside her, she would be as right as rain. She knew one could be addicted to tea or coffee; they both contained certain amounts of caffeine, but as to being addictive, her answer was – 'a definite yes'.

Crawford had been talking to Silas Kefford to check on the day's weather before returning to the breakfast table. 'Lizzie', he asked, 'you look well?' At least Crawford had the decency to check on my health and displayed immaculate manners when conversing with members of the opposite sex – unlike Lord Bloody Hill.

Lizzie bit her tongue; she didn't want to lose any of her self-control. She smiled sweetly at both men and, without harping on the matter of sleepless nights, she informed them that she had slept well. 'I feel ready to face the day. If you two gentlemen intend to go out, I think I will stay here and gossip with Julia and Hestia', she declared.

Before either man vacated the breakfast table, she enquired if Crawford knew of the expression 'Memento Mori'; she knew, of course, that it was Latin. Without taking time in thinking of his answer Crawford told her, 'It means *remember you too will die*. Why do you ask?'

How could she explain to Crawford how these words mysteriously appeared out of nowhere, written by an unseen hand on her bedroom window. Instead, she told him, 'It just popped into my head, maybe I saw it on one of the churchyard gravestones'.

'Damn funny thing to pop into your head Lizzie, perhaps you shouldn't eat as much cheese last thing at night'.

Remember you too will die

CHAPTER 11

Knowledge and Revelations

Crawford and Hill decided it was only proper they should pay their respects to the Salisbury family, but Lizzie thought their true aim was to seek out clues, especially something that the police or fire service might have overlooked; not that they expected to find much, the fire's point of origin had been acknowledged to be with the Dowager's personal quarters, or, to be more precise, her bedroom. The fire had completely destroyed the private chapel together with much of the west wing, the pungent smell of acrid smouldering timbers, burnt plaster and scorched stone. Thick, muddy slurry covered most of the ground floor in the west wing, courtesy of the disintegrating water tank high up in the rafters. It might have saved the fire from spreading to other parts of the house, but it made searching for clues nearly impossible. Both men thought it worthwhile to risk wasting time to search for clues; if any had been any; they most certainly would have evaporated along with the Dowager's jewellery.

Meanwhile, Lizzie bid her time waiting for the right moment to speak to Julia and her daughter. She wanted to talk to them together, away for Silas. She thought she would study their body language by skirting around the peripheries of the bar before allowing herself to gradually spiral inwards to invade their personal space. Lizzie was an excellent student at school, gaining full marks in most subjects; she particularly excelled in natural history and evolutionary biology, studying the process that produced the diversity of life on Earth. From her early teenage years, she had enjoyed the simplistic curls of the ammonite fossils that symbolised the continuing changes in evolution. As a young child she had been mesmerized by the way all fossils absorbed cosmic energy over millions of years helping to stimulate a life force. Before people fully understood fossilisation and evolution, their curious patterns and shapes were often explained through folk tales and myths. The ancient Greeks believed that the bones of mammoths and dinosaurs originated from giants, relics from a time when giants ruled the world, but Lizzie knew better. Everyone knew Lizzie was a bright child, always ready with a question and thirst for knowledge; sadly, she didn't have that many friends – if anything, she was a lonely child.

Lord Hill often wondered why Crawford was protective towards Lizzie. Their relationship seemed comfortable, not in a sexual way; it was more like father and daughter. Hill knew that Crawford's wife was alive, but he also knew they hadn't had the good fortune of being able to conceive children, unless Lizzie was a love-child born out of wedlock, but that didn't make sense as John Crawford had been a true and faithful husband and his wife had always doted on him. He quickly discounted the thought of Lizzie being a love-child; all the same, there was some extreme closeness between the two of them. 'One day', Hill thought, 'if he wants to tell me, he will'.

Julia and Hestia sat by one of the tables deep in conversation. Lizzie was unsure where Silas was; all she knew was if she was quick, she could gain their trust if only she could converse with them. Lizzie slowly circled them, careful not to appear menacing or threatening. She made sure her posture and facial expressions all appeared natural as she hoped to build a relationship with both women. She needed the Keffords to be relaxed and required both of them to her trust, as she planned to unravel their secrets. Lizzie needed an excuse to get one of the women to start an innocent conversation – that would be her way in!

She was very close, no more than a few feet away from Hestia when Lizzie started humming nonchalantly. She felt confident that Hestia knew the Christmas carol, and as luck would have it, she did even though it was relatively new, and what was more, she joined in the familiar chorus line.

Silent night, holy night
All is calm, all is bright.
Round yon Virgin, Mother and child
Holy infant so tender and mild.
Sleep in heavenly peace,
Sleep in heavenly peace.
Silent night, holy night,
Shepherds quake at the sight
Glories stream from heaven afar,
Heavenly hosts sing Alleluia!
Christ, the saviour is born,
Christ, the saviour is born.
Silent night, holy night

Son of God, love's pure light.
Radiant beams from Thy Holy face
With the dawn of redeeming grace
Jesus, Lord, at Thy birth,
Jesus, Lord, at Thy birth.

'It's one of my favourites', Hestia replied. 'Mother used to sing it to me when I was younger. Do you know it was originally written as a poem by an Austrian priest not long after the great battle at Waterloo? As time went by, the lyrics became so poignant that it evolved into a fashionable Christmas carol'. She continued, 'They tell me Victoria looks kindly on the song.' Lizzie wasn't aware if the carol gained favour with the queen or not; what was important to Lizzie was that she had wormed her way into a conversation. The door had been opened, which gave her a legitimate excuse to sit with the Keffords. Lizzie's brain was working furiously as she studied the manncrisms of both women; the riddle she needed to solve was whether one of them was capable of murder, or had they joined forces to kill and commit arson? Lizzie knew that one of them was guarding a deep black secret, but she didn't know which one. She was aware that her mind was purposely being blocked by one of them – which one was it?

The Keffords externally appeared relaxed, but Lizzie knew from experience from their body language that both women were desperate to conceal a terrible secret, which led to one of them to turn to murder, but which one and what was the secret?

Lizzie informed Hestia and Julia Kefford that she had worked in some of London's famous theatres, entertaining the audiences with her mind-reading act. Hestia's reaction was one of excitement, whilst Julia appeared nervous; eventually Hestia pressurised her mother into consenting in letting Lizzie entertain them while they waited for Silas to return.

Hestia giggled and started to bite her nails as Lizzie commenced,; Lizzie noticed Hestia's nails had been regularly nibbled and chewed, probably as a result of an obsessive compulsive grooming disorder similar to other anxiety related habits, such as hair touching or fidgety fingers, both of which were prevalent in Hestia.

Lizzie considered using her old parlour game skills to unlock Hestia's mind. With little to lose, she set about her task by exaggerating her well-rehearsed trance-like condition; she had practiced this many times in the past with amazing results. She just needed to convince Hestia and Julia that her abilities in contacting the spirit world was authentic. She had always maintained her act, for that was what it was – it was just for entertainment. She would never shock anyone by delivering horrific news. She felt nervous as she went about her duties of convincing Hestia that she was a genuine medium, capable of speaking to the dead. Part of her told her it was all humbug, whilst the other part told her it was important to ascertain the truth.

Lizzie wasn't going to predict the future; that was against a true medium's code of practice. She aimed her strategy at unlocking the past. She stood erect, closed her eyes, breathed deeply, and turned her head one way and the other as if concentrating on some sort of manifestation. She told the Keffords, 'I have a lady here who is trying to communicate with me – the lady's name is Louisa or Louise – she is desperately trying to get my attention by tugging at my sleeve'. Lizzie opened her eyes for no other reason than to check on any reactions, especially from Julia, but seeing none she reclosed her eyes and continued with her performance. 'Does the name Louisa mean anything to either of you?' she repeated. Both women told Lizzie that the name meant nothing.

Lizzie was conscious of their deception! Additionally, Lizzie was aware Juliette's, or Julia's, as she preferred to call herself, mother's name was Louisa. Hill had already explained this fact, so she perused this weak point by confirming the name Louisa. She would not budge from this, 'My name is Louisa. Why did you forsake the name I gave you?' That brought a reaction from both women; she now held their full attention.

As if to reiterate the point, Lizzie repeated herself, 'My name is Louisa, I am from England, I teach children, I married a man from Belgium called Jacque, his name is Norman or Normaine or Noureddine'. Although Julia was trembling, she allowed Lizzie to continue with her act, hoping to prove she had the story wrong. Lizzie was just about to deliver her pièce de résistance, when Julia unexpectedly called out in anguish, 'I'm so sorry, mother'. By now, Lizzie was supremely confident that Julia and Juliette Kefford were one and the same person, but she had to be careful not to push Julia Kefford too hard; in addition, she was certain she had Julia eating out of her hands. Perhaps one more revelation would do the trick. Julia was in tears, unhappy and insecure., Lizzie needed to continue with extreme caution if she was to fully open Julia's mind – she took a chance. Lizzie Drew shouted at the top of her voice the one word which brought Julia Kefford to her feet. 'Fire'. She shouted again, 'Burning'. Misses Kefford was crying uncontrollably, and Lizzie knew she had successfully unlocked Pandora's Box, which revealed nothing other than darkness and misery.

With the identity of Julia and Thomas Aston, and the word 'fire', Julia ran from the table into the direction of her kitchen, leaving her daughter to wonder if she should follow or remain where she was. Hestia decided to stay and apologised on behalf of her mother, 'I'm sorry I don't know what's got into mother'. As Silas returned, she heard his panic-stricken wife's frenzied cries resonating from the kitchen and demanded to know what had happened. Hestia remained calm and told her father they were just having a bit of fun. Lizzie was talking to the spirits.

'I'm sorry, Mr. Kefford, it was not my intention to frighten or scare your wife in any way. We were simply having fun until you returned. I informed your wife and daughter of my distinctive talents when I became aware of a message from a Juliette and Thomas Aston connected to a fire'. Silas remained transfixed and traumatised. He ordered his daughter to go and attend to her mother; he lowered his voice and cautioned Lizzie, 'I don't want any pagan ceremonies going on in my house'.

Hestia found her mother cowering by the kitchen stove. She was weeping hysterically, completely out of control. Hestia knew she had just witnessed something strange but was unable to comprehend her mother's anguish. Silas tried to console his wife with an embrace, but she pushed her husband away; Lizzie had opened the Box only to find it void of happiness; all she had discovered was tragedy and foreboding. If Lizzie was a gambler, she still didn't know where to place her bet with regard to who the guilty party was – perhaps all three were guilty, but then again perhaps they were all innocent. She couldn't continue. Her performance had brought nothing but heartbreak beyond her imagination. As she peered into the kitchen, she asked to speak to Mister Kefford privately.

Reluctantly, Silas Kefford slowly ambled back to speak with Lizzie. 'Hestia is such a beautiful name, I wonder if you could explain its origin'. Silas considered if the question was another of Lizzie's tricks, but seeing naught to deceive him, he inhaled, sucked his lips inwardly, as if pulling a disgruntled face and answered. 'It is my understanding the name originates from either Roman or Greek mythology. My brother-in-law suggested the name to my wife, and she loved it. I had no say in it; I have no idea where the name originates from except to say that my daughter is beautiful, and Hestia is an unusual and attractive name. It's just a name with no signification'. Lizzie nodded her approval, 'Yes, Mister Kefford, I agree, it is a beautiful name for a beautiful girl. Once again, please pass on my apologies to your wife for any upset caused; it was not intended'. Silas returned to the kitchen to his wife and daughter looking utterly crestfallen. If Silas Kefford was acting, he was most adept in his performance.

Crawford and Hill had already informed Lizzie that private Kefford had entered the church and saved a young girl and her uncle from certain death. She presumed the young girl was Juliette or Julia, and Kefford was none other than the landlord of the Eight Bells; that much appeared obvious. The fire had apparently been started deliberately by a drunk and conceited Captain Boyd, who had fled the atrocity only to be murdered himself soon after. That much seemed clear. Lizzie had two questions for Crawford upon his return to Hatfield: the origin of the name Hestia and the identity of Julia's mysterious uncle. Did they jointly return to England following the massacre at Sombreffe?

When Crawford returned and Lizzie explained her story, he had a question for her. 'Why on earth did you tell the Keffords about a Julia and Thomas Aston, a brother and sister who remained in Belgium to help the poor residents of Sombreffe, when the name has never been revealed to neither Hill nor me?'

Lizzie was shocked. The names hadn't been revealed, so how did she know them? Had her sixth-sense been released?

CHAPTER 12

Greek & Cholera
(An unlikely combination)

Standing outside the Eight Bells, Lizzie felt chilly but remained bewildered by Crawford's initial response with her performance with the Keffords. She had no idea where the name Aston had come from. She eagerly awaited Crawford and Hill to finish their evening meal to join her and hopefully explain the symbolism behind Kefford's daughter's unusual name. Lizzie had a hunch that it could prove relevant in understanding what happened at Sombreffe and Hatfield House. She also wondered if Lord Hill had managed to uncover any new information that might throw light on her assuming Aston was important to their investigation.

It was gone nine o'clock before Lizzie was joined by her two colleagues. She greeted them enthusiastically as she looked towards the heavens and noticed that daylight had long been overtaken by a star-filled night sky. The stars, thanks to a cloudless night, were shining bright above. Lizzie had been deep in thought, waiting to be educated on Roman or Greek mythology by her knowledgeable God-father. No wonder she felt chilly – a cloudless night meant low temperatures.

Crawford, unlike Hill, felt the cold, but tonight both men appeared happy and relaxed, especially after their earlier talk with Lizzie. She had briefed them about her interactions with the Keffords, but she held off seeking answers to her questions until Hill finished smoking his pipe. She wanted their full attention.

Now that she had both men's attention, she spoke of her assumptions that the Kefford family were involved in some manner with the numerous arson attacks, but as to which one she could not tell. She knew John Crawford to be knowledgeable on most subjects and hoped mythology was one of them.

'Before we go back inside, can you please enlighten me about the origin of Hestia's name?' she asked.

Crawford was surprised why she had asked the question, but as he answering he began to realise where her thoughts were directing him. 'I did study Greek and Roman mythology at Cambridge. If I recall the name, Hestia is closely associated with Greek mythology as opposed to Roman. It's connected to the hearth, fireplace, or alter. It seems from the same root as the English verbal form of *to live*, or *dwell and pass through the night*; it thus refers to the oikos within the household or family. An early form of Hestia's temple was called the hearth house; the temples at Dreros and Prinias on the island of Crete were of this type as was the temple of Apollo at Delphi, all of which had an inner Hestia. The Mycenaean Great Hall or megaron, like Homer's Hall of Odysseus at Ithaca, had a central hearth. Likewise,

157

the hearth of the later Greek prytaneum was for the community as well as for the government's ritual and secular focuses.

Both Hill and Lizzie looked dumbstruck and asked Crawford to repeat his explanation in plain English.

Crawford thought long and hard how to respond and to make sure Lizzie and Hill understood his explanations. 'Basically, Hestia's name and functions signify the hearth's importance in the social, religious and political life within Greek culture. As the hearth is essential for warmth, food preparation and the completion of sacrificial offerings to the deities, during sacrifices Hestia was the customary recipient of usually cheap offerings. She was also offered the first and last libations of wine during the feats. Hestia's sacrificial animal was the domestic pig, and the accidental or negligent extinction of the hearth-fire represented a failure of domestic and religious duties to the family. Failure to main Hestia's fire in her temple or shrine was a breach of duty of the community'.

Lizzie interrupted Crawford by attempting clarification of what had just been elucidated. 'If a hearth fire was deliberately extinguished, its lighting or relighting should be accompanied by rituals, purifications and renewal'.

'Yes, with the rituals and connotations of an eternal flame or sanctuary lamps throughout the Greek colonies, their mother cities were allied and sanctified through Hestia's cult. Hestia's nearest

Roman equivalent is Vesta; she had a similar role as a divine Roman acknowledgement binding Romans together around the hearth-fire'.

Lizzie looked at Crawford in utter amazement. How the hell did he remember all that information without first revising was beyond her. She knew Crawford to be in his early seventies. When he had left Cambridge with his degrees, he must have been no more than twenty-five – that was around forty-five years ago. Lizzie found it difficult to remember what she had eaten for breakfast. For Crawford to instantly recall Greek mythology after nearly half a century was both astonishing and amazing.

'Okay', she replied. 'What you're telling us is that Hestia has significant significations with fire, or have I completely missed the point?'

Hill shifted from one foot to the other trying to keep warm. 'Don't mind me', he said, 'now I know the meaning behind two's company and three's a crowd, but I still don't know what you two have been barking on about during the past half-hour'. Lizzie and Crawford glanced at each other in total amazement before laughing at Hill's stupidity.

'Surely you can see the correlation with Hestia's unusual forename and fire. Do you think the choice of name is both bizarre and coincidental? Her name was not chosen for her by her parents; it was her uncle's idea'. Lizzie considered asking Lord Hill if he had anything to add but thought better of it. Hill was a dear man; if not a shade eccentric, he could be rude and discourteous and in the blink of an eye be polite and courteous – all of it depended on which side of the bed he got out of.

Crawford curled his wispy beard between his thumb and forefinger on his right hand before suggesting that he and Lizzie should question Silas and Julia, preferably without Hestia's presence, whilst Hill thought he might return to Horse Guards to ascertain if he could bribe someone to help him view any classified information appertaining to the Sombreffe massacre.

The last coach to London left Hatfield around eleven o'clock, which gave Hill ample time to enjoy a couple of pints before the coach left. 'I should return mid-morning the day after tomorrow. Wish me luck!'

Without Hill around for a full day, Crawford hoped it would enable him to renew his association with Lizzie and her family. He was particularly interested to know how her family had fared over the years. The last time he had been with her family was at Lizzie's wedding where, once again, he was unable to stay for the festivities due to business commitments. He knew her father, the Honourable Lord Sudbury, had links to the river Thames as a major importer of timber, and it was within the ports of Great Britain where various deadly diseases claimed the majority of its victims. What he didn't know was whether her parents had survived the recent cholera epidemics that had blighted the ports throughout the past eight years. The first significant incident of the highly contagious bacterial disease took place in Sunderland, on the north-east coast of England, in October 1831, when a vessel from the

Baltic region with sick sailors aboard docked within the port. The ship was apparently allowed to dock because the port authorities either objected or ignored government instructions to quarantine every vessel coming from the Baltic States. The disease quickly spread from Sunderland northwards to Scotland and southwards towards London. Before it run its course, cholera had claimed more than 52000 innocent victims. Its beginnings were in the sub-continent of India and took five years to creep into Europe. Thus, by the time it reached Sunderland, British doctors were well aware of the fatalities the disease brought, but no one knew how to prevent the spread of the deadly disease. During those early days, to be infected with cholera was a death sentence; doctors couldn't do anything other than make patients comfortable and watch helplessly as they died.

Crawford knew the symptoms of cholera only too well from his army and diplomatic days, and it wasn't pleasant to witness – bouts of giddiness, sickness, nervous agitation, intermittent slow or weak pulse, severe cramps starting at the tips of the fingers and toes and rapidly affecting the torso, and that was just the beginning. Vomiting and purging of all liquids followed before the patient's facial features contracted, eyes withdrew into their sockets to give an impression of terror and wildness; finally their lips, face, neck, hands, thighs, arms and skin assumed a leaden blue, purple, black or deep brown tint, depending on the original complexion of the individual. Their fingers and toes reduced in size, their skin and soft tissue became wrinkled, shrivelled and folded. The nails turned a bluish-pearly white, the larger superficial veins became marked by flat lines of deeper black, the pulse became as small as a thread of cotton before disappearing. Crawford shuddered as he thought about the complacency with which the dock workers initially regarded the disease, but once they died in the hundreds, anxiety and fear gripped the workforce and their dependents.

Crawford forced himself to erase from his mind every thought of sickness and disease; he simply hoped her parents were alive and well and thought about how they had coped with a feisty daughter like Lizzie.

Lizzie enjoyed chatting with her god-father; it felt good to reflect on happier times when her parents and Crawford and his wife entertained the children with stories of how the world was rapidly changing, and what the young expected as opposed to their parents. Everything was rosy in Lizzie's life – her childhood, education and her transformation into womanhood was delightful. She knew of the squalled lives of the unfortunates and hoped one day to be able to make a difference to their standards and living conditions; perhaps if women held the power to change things, things would be different, but at present they were looked upon as nothing more than breeding machines.

'Lizzie', Crawford abruptly stopped her in mid-conversation, 'You sound like a radical'. 'If I do, it's only because I care, I want to make a difference'.

Noticing Silas behind the bar, Crawford called out, 'Excellent meal tonight, Mister Kefford, please commend your wife on her excellent cooking skills. I have never tasted roast beef as your good lady prepared this evening – a culinary delight'. Silas looked confused; perhaps he didn't understand the term *culinary delight*, or maybe he had other matters on his mind.

'Sorry Silas, I forgot to mention that Lord Hill has had to return to London. Only two for breakfast in the morning, if you please'. Silas nodded and thanked Crawford for his compliments, but Lizzie was unsure if she should converse with Mister Kefford. After all it was her trickery that had so upset his wife. She thought the ice had to be broken. 'Mister Kefford, please apologise to your wife one my behalf if I upset her last afternoon. That was never my intention; things just got out of hand. I can assure you I am not a fortune-teller. If anything, I try to glimpse the past; I can only see what my guide wishes me to see, and sometimes they get it wrong'.

Silas, without looking at his guests, nodded before wishing them both a good night. 'A good night to you', Crawford yawned to exaggerate his tiredness and escorted Lizzie to her room.

CHAPTER 13

Arsonists & Butterflies

After breakfast the following morning, Crawford and Lizzie decided they needed to get away from Hatfield for the day to clear their heads of recent events. Richard's body had been reunited with his family at Northfleet in the county of Kent; they had sent a letter back to Crawford, thanking him for his financial help with the burial costs and inviting him, along with any of Richard's friends from his new employment, to his wake on Friday, the fifteenth day of December.

Crawford was satisfied that Richard Briggs' burial would take place before Hogmanay. Being a Scotsman, he reminded Lizzie of his native superstitions, especially about the traditions of first-footing. He told her to make sure she was debt-free before the first day of January, otherwise she would be paying money all year. Another one of his traditions was never to lend money on New Year's Day. According to him, to do so guaranteed that you'll be paying out all year. Lizzie speculated upon this so-called tradition. She had known Crawford to never lend money on any day of the year. She explained to her godfather about one of her superstitions concerning white butterflies. 'If you see one on the first of January', she explained, 'it's considered a good omen'.

Crawford cut her off abruptly by saying there was no such thing as a pure white butterfly, which brought a look of horror to Lizzie's face. Crawford giggled as he confirmed he had also heard about the old wives' tale about white butterflies. 'Technically speaking,' he said, 'they're not butterflies – they're moths.'

Crawford apologised for having his bit of fun at Lizzie's expense and suggested they should go to a nearby village. 'We have lots to catch-up on, particularly about your family, who I trust are well. I hear Bramfield is a particularly pretty village with a lovely little village green when it is not raining, and today it ain't raining.' Having hired a small pony and trap, Lizzie and Crawford arrived in Bramfield just after one o'clock. The pair were taken aback by the sheer quaintness of the village, with its little church and village green complete with its own little pond. Crawford remembered Bramfield from his days at Cambridge, that Thomas Becket was reputed to have brewed his own ale using water from the pond prior to his rise to Archbishop of Canterbury.

Crawford suggested they enjoy a wee dram at the Grandison before Lizzie shared her story. After a couple of drinks, Crawford made himself comfortable by the open fireplace in readiness for Lizzie's life story. Her parents were alive and lived at Sudbury in the county of Suffolk; her father had been in the timber trade, importing large quantities of pine and deal from Scandinavia to the newly constructed Surrey Docks along the south bank of the Thames at Southwark. With regards to herself, she had married twice, once to a scoundrel who had died young due to his excessive drinking, and now she was happily married to her second husband. Lizzie had always trod an adventurous tom-boyish path that she found well-suited to her present employment with Crawford.

Lizzie hadn't seen him for nearly twenty years, but she always remembered her Uncle John for generosity, especially on Christmas and birthdays. 'I think your smile has removed all feelings of guilt from my head, although as the commander of the agency, I do blame myself for Richard's murder. But I am certain we will soon bring his killer to justice,' Crawford said in a sullen tone. Lizzie said nothing and simply nodded to show her agreement with his last statement. 'We must be ready with our line of questioning; I know you have sincere misgivings concerning the guilt of the Keffords, but at present, they are our only suspects.' Crawford was writing notes whilst talking to Lizzie.

Lizzie asked Crawford if he had ever considered the murder of Richard Briggs and the recent arson attacks at Westminster and Hatfield to be the work of one person or a group. Crawford did have peculiar habits when trying to concentrate; this time he tapped his fingers on the table in tune with the National Anthem of France, La Marseillaise. Lizzie just hoped her godfather wouldn't burst into song. Crawford explained to his goddaughter that after France declared war on Austria on the twentieth of April, 1792, the mayor of Strasbourg, where the composer Rouget de Lisle was billeted. Napoleon expressed the need for a jolly marching song to inspire the French troops. 'La Marseillaise' was

Rouget de Lisle's response to this call. The song had only been reintroduced in French culture after the July revolution of 1830, but it was muted that Napoleon III intended to ban the anthem in favour of something else.

Lizzie thought Crawford secretly liked the song, but at the same time, it created fear in his heart. He had probably heard the song too many times on numerous battlefields across Europe and North Africa. Crawford handed Lizzie a list of questions he wished her to put before Silas and Julia Kefford, and in brackets at the end of each question, he indicated whether the question should be asked quietly or forcibly, in appeasement or in an antagonistic manner. He didn't want Hestia to be present during the interview; her questioning would follow depending on what her parents had to offer.

Lizzie turned to look at Crawford, 'Are you sure that the only way to progress is to question the daughter without her parents being present? That sounds cruel'. Crawford replied, 'To murder Richard Briggs was merciless'. Lizzie reluctantly agreed to his suggestion and asked which questions were for her to ask and which ones was Crawford going to raise. He replied, 'You're the questioner – I'll be there simply to listen to the replies.' He quickly added a footnote for Lizzie and said, 'If you feel at any time during the questioning that something is not right, or if an additional question could be beneficial, please push your inquiring mind harder.'

Crawford finished his tactical talk by saying, 'Do it for Richard'.

'Best get back to the Eight Bells, Hilly might be back by now,' Lizzie declared. On their way back to Hatfield, Lizzie inquired if Crawford had any ideas why the arsonist set the first fire in Hatfield. She told herself it wasn't for financial gain and wondered if the arsonist would commit the crime whilst being in a highly emotional state, possibly under the influence of alcohol. It was possible that this individual set the fires in bedrooms or in storerooms in an attempt to destroy personal possessions of sentimental value belonging to the victims, just like the Dowager and at the Houses of Parliament. She honestly thought that the perpetrator had no intention of committing murder; the death of the Dowager had been accidental, but the fire had been planned in advance – presumably the Dowagers death was a side issue caused solely by the lady's age; her death was not intended. The fire at Westminster had aroused the arsonist; he or she had acquired their revenge in a most spectacular fashion, without loss of life, and that was what the arsonists wanted. He or she had made Parliament sit up and take notice. Lizzie speculated as to why the Prime Minister had been targeted: had it been an act against the idea of Prime Ministers or against the head of state a figurehead? Or was it an act against the nation? If her assumptions were correct, she wanted England to lose something, probably its status of being the focal point in terms of time, navigation and prestige.

Arsonists who set fires to conceal a previous crime probably are the least interested in the phenomenon of fire itself, unless a fire had destroyed their life. These arsonists simply crave the destruction of any physical evidence or to divert attention from another crime, and a fire is a handy weapon for doing exactly that. Lizzie discounted the arsonist being adolescent, starting fires as a means to excite or to relieve boredom, with uncomplicated, crude devices, as these fires were routinely accompanied by vandalism and theft. On their way back to the village of Hatfield, Lizzie updated Crawford on her various theories to see if any of it made sense to him.

Crawford agreed that this arsonist fitted the profile of a person seeking revenge against the establishment; the fires were not the work of an individual intent to steal or vandalise. He liked the idea of revenge to cover-up an earlier crime; what he couldn't understand was why Briggs had to be killed? Unless the person responsible thought they were getting too close to unravelling the truth – or was someone protecting the perpetrator of the crimes?

'That makes sense, John', she told him.

'We're nearly back at Hatfield, Lizzie. Best not call me 'Uncle' anymore. I'm going to remove all affiliations to you from my life. I don't want you to become a target of this insane arsonist because of your connection to me.'

'Okay, Uncle,' Lizzie joked, but it was no joke.

CHAPTER 14

Have We a Name!

Daylight was fading fast when Crawford and Lizzie returned to Hatfield, where they were in for a most pleasant surprise. Not only was Hill waiting for them, but Sam Vickers was standing by his side. Hill had an enormous grin spread from ear to ear as Crawford carefully descended from his hired pony and trap; Lizzie smiled, pleased to see Samuel.

'I've already updated Samuel on Richard's death, but I have something of far greater significance', Hill said as he waved a sheaf of paper in his hand. 'This will warm the cockles of your heart, John', he proclaimed, as if one sheet of paper had solved a crime that had proved so difficult to understand.

Crawford seemed to realise the importance of what Hill had been trying to explain and suggested that all four should meet in private in Crawford's room. 'Come upstairs, gentlemen', which left Lizzie somewhat bemused when she responded; 'Shall I stay here or join you men?'

'Sorry Lizzie, no offence'. 'None taken, sir', she replied somewhat sarcastically. Crawford didn't like derision and made sure by his raised eyebrow gesture that Lizzie knew it.

As everyone ascended the stairs, Lizzie noticed Silas Kefford watching them from behind his bar. She thought it better to say something rather than smile or wave. 'Just going to change our clothes and be down shortly for our evening meal. We have one extra for dinner tonight, hope that's okay with you, Mister Kefford'.

'I suppose it will have to be, but be quick, your food will be on the table in ten minutes, and if you're not here, I'll feed it to the dogs,' Kefford replied with irritation ringing in his voice before speedily vanishing into the kitchen. 'O dear, someone's upset him', Lizzie declared.

Once Crawford's team were safely inside his room, Hill explained the additional information, which up until a few days ago had been deemed as sensitive or classified material. 'For the benefit of everyone', Hill continued, 'it means that if disclosed, this will cause embarrassment to our government or the armed forces. It seems that Captain Boyd was murdered by a man who lived in Sombreffe, and not by Polish Lancers as previously thought. It seems the motive was to revenge the murder of his sister, and principally the rape of his niece.'

Crawford demanded to know if Hill had indisputable proof or if this was simply hearsay. 'I have the official document here in black and white.'

'Have we a name?' Crawford asked again, getting extremely impatient.

Hill quickly responded, 'Yes, I found a name'. 'And?' Crawford's impatience was building. Hill paused to foster the suspense, to Crawford's obvious annoyance. 'His name was Thomas Aston.'

Crawford stared at Lizzie in disbelief, 'How could you possibly have known this name prior to Hill's meeting at Horse Guards?' Lizzie was totally bewildered. 'I cannot explain', she replied, 'unless...' 'Unless what?' Crawford queried.

Crawford was anxious to know what else Hill had gleaned from the Horse Guards. Hill quickly regained his composure. 'Within Kefford's file, his senior officer recorded his permission to marry Juliette Noureddine, daughter of Jacque and Louisa Noureddine, both deceased – an under-age pregnant girl from Sombreffe. The documentation was counter-signed by a Thomas Aston, brother to Louisa Noureddine and uncle of the girl'.

'It appears the Provost Marshal's decided to not take further action against Thomas Aston, the prime suspect in Boyd's murder, due to the atrocities inflicted when over twenty men, women, and children were murdered by Captain Boyd's men inside Sombreffe chapel, a place of sanctuary. Apparently the villagers and Boyd's men had been drinking heavily throughout the night, and without reliable witnesses coming forward, the case was marked as "unproved"; however, the offence of rape against the girl was proved, and Boyd was sentenced to be executed at dawn the following morning, and we all know the rest'.

'There's more', Hill continued. 'Two witnesses did testify that the fire started within the chapel after the villagers were secured inside, but as this didn't appear to match with other eye-witness accounts, their statements were erased from the trial'.

'You know what this means', Vickers explained. 'If true, it means that Boyd couldn't have started the fire that killed all those people; he was outside, probably in a state of drunken stupor'.

Sam asked, 'Do we know what happened to Thomas Aston after Waterloo? Did he remain in Belgium or return to England with Kefford?'

'According to my intelligence reports', Hill continued, 'I cannot be sure, but I *can* confirm that one of the witnesses at Silas's marriage was Thomas Aston.'

Crawford thought that interesting. Although he had already guessed the answer, he asked the question all the same, 'Where did the couple marry?'

'Right here, at St. Etheldreda's,' Hill replied. 'The church on top of the hill, the late Reverend Boyd's church'.

'Okay', Crawford continued. 'We have a name, and we know Thomas Aston returned to England about the same time as Silas Kefford. I wager any money you care to mention: the father of Julia's child was none other than Captain Edward Boyd. He brought shame upon the Noureddine family. Private Silas Kefford couldn't have been involved as he was only in Sombreffe for less than an hour, whereas Boyd was stationed there for over a month as a part of Wellington's reconnaissance troupe'.

Crawford was confident he was close to solving the mystery. 'We know Silas, Julia, and Hestia Kefford cannot be the murders; they were all under our observation, they never left this place. In addition, when Parliament went up in flames, the Keffords didn't stray too far from Hatfield'.

'I sent a message to the Prime Minister via Willie, asking him if Downing Street ever hired casual staff, and I have his reply right here. In the past five years, the Prime Minister's office only engaged fourteen casual staff, but if you compare that list with part-time staff employed at the Houses of Parliament, only two names appear on both lists: one was an elderly woman and the other was a Thomas Aston from Hertfordshire'.

Hill wasn't overly surprised. From the information he had already gained from Horse Guards, he knew the common denominator to be Thomas Aston. 'But who was he and where is he now?' Hill asked with a hint of desperation in his voice.

Crawford looked at Hill in amazement, 'I think you will find that the last time you set eyes on him, you foolhardily placed a bet on his dog.'

Lizzie broke into the conversation. 'I can understand him having a deep hatred against the Boyd family, but why take it further and risk being caught by taking his revenge out against Parliament and Earl Grey?'

Crawford was happy to respond to Lizzie's question by confirming that one additional fact that could be used in evidence against Thomas Aston hadn't been accepted. He explained, 'According to the medical reports following the carnage at Sombreffe, one of the survivors, a Mister Thomas Aston, had his left foot amputated due to severe burns. If you recall, the footman at Downing Street walked with a cane due to a foot injury, and the old man who nightly walked his dog into the Eight Bells had to walk with a cane. Thomas Aston has been in plain sight throughout our investigation, as he told us'.

'Bloody hell!' Lizzie squirmed. 'You're right'.

Crawford wanted to expose Thomas Aston to the Keffords as a murder and arsonist straight away but suggested they should have a quiet talk to them first. 'We will discuss this over dinner'.

'How do you think the Keffords will take it?' Lizzie enquired. Crawford knew Julia Kefford wouldn't accept the fact that her uncle was the prime suspect in the recent arson attacks.

The team sat down and waited patiently for Julia Kefford to serve the evening meal. Crawford enquired if her husband and daughter were in the kitchen, as he wished to impart significant information to the family.

Once Silas and Hestia had joined Julia at the table, Crawford began the explanation by stating that he was the commander of an elite diplomatic department initiated by the Prime Minister to protect the monarchy and politicians from any unforeseen harm. 'As you are aware, there have been a number of recent arson attacks, and my team is convinced that Thomas Aston is guilty of the crime'. Silas couldn't believe what he was hearing. 'Thomas is a gentle man; he wouldn't harm a fly. I don't believe it, you are most mistaken'. Crawford explained his evidence surrounding Aston's guilt; he had been employed at Downing Street and the Houses of Parliament, he had no alibi for his whereabouts when the big house was set alight, he was at Sombreffe when Boyd raped Julia Noureddine. Crawford turned to look at Hestia and dreaded what he was about to suggest 'He was at Hatfield when the Reverend Boyd was murdered at the vicarage'. Hestia screamed in panic and had to be consoled by her mother, who hissed violently at Crawford. 'That evil vicar spawned one evil bastard; it was his son who murdered my mother and father, along with others at Sombreffe. That vicar deserved to die'. Lizzie remained calm. 'You do understand that the fire started inside the church'. 'Yes, by Captain Boyd', Julia screamed. 'That has yet to be proved', Crawford explained, trying to keep tempers under control.

'You have my sincere apologies for the dishonourable behaviour from an officer of the British army, none should stoop so low as to inflict so much pain and agony on the very people they should have been protecting – men, women and children', Crawford was near to tears as he carried on speaking.

'However, we now have other killings to be reconciled, like that of the Reverend William Edward Boyd as well as one of my team and the Dowager Marchioness'. At the mention of the reverend's name, Hestia collapsed and burst into tears.

'Fuck your sincerities, they mean nothing, you have gravely upset my daughter'. Silas was getting ready for a fight, but it was Hestia who appeared to be the most offended, especially when Hill weighed in with his comment. 'I'm afraid there's much doubt who your father is, Miss Kefford'.

Hestia grief stricken, both for herself and the reverend, she remembered speaking to her Uncle Thomas of her pain when her parents had told her the truth about her parentage. The man she had called 'Father' all these years had not been her true biological father, but she would always recognise and love Silas Kefford as her father. It was he who had married her mother to make sure tongues didn't wag, to make sure fingers were not pointed, and to make sure Hestia had a righteous and good upbringing. She didn't know if the vicar at St. Etheldreda knew the truth about her parentage – she thought not. All Hestia knew was that the reverend was a decent man and didn't deserve to die. She had confided in her uncle and even suggested to him that she didn't want to see another member of the Boyd family. Shortly after her private conversation, the reverend was dead, killed in a fire at his house. She never considered her uncle played any part in the reverend's death, which was nothing more than ridiculous speculation.

Silas Kefford spoke next. Slowly calming down, he seemed unable to come to terms with what had been speculated. 'I cannot believe what you are insinuating. Thomas was always a good man, but after Sombreffe, he changed. He was no longer the man I knew. He criticised me for not seeking revenge against those who dishonoured his family'.

'He told me the French killed Boyd. He gave me the money found on Boyd's body. He helped me to buy this place. I cannot believe he's a killer – I will not!'

Julia Kefford remained silent, her eyes transfixed on some obscure point on the ceiling in front of her. She was in shock – Silas tried to comfort her.

Crawford tried to explain to Silas that the attack on the Houses of Parliament and at Hatfield House was the work of Thomas. It seems he was working alone in an attempt to make the British Government suffer. 'I can only assume he was trying to punish the government and others he held responsible for the wrongs he felt they carried out. In his own bizarre way, he was trying to set the record straight; he was wrong, and his actions cannot be condoned'. Samuel Vickers enquired if they knew where Aston might be, and Silas replied, 'My brother-in-law left for London yesterday morning. He had an appointment at Lloyd's, that's all I know.'

'I'm sorry to inform you that Thomas probably intends to start another fire; do you know which Lloyd's establishment he intended to visit?'

Crawford was frantic as he shouted at Silas Kefford. 'I cannot put it any clearer. Innocent lives are at stake! Sod the buildings, they are insured.'

'That's it', Lizzie exclaimed, 'Lloyd's of London, the insurance company. That must be his target!'

'Silas, I beg you', Crawford pleaded, 'if Thomas tries to contact you, please send me a message at this address at Whitehall.'

Silas told Crawford there would be no coaches travelling to London until eight in the next morning. Hill contacted the mail office and booked four tickets with the coach company, who assured him that no matter what, his tickets were guaranteed, and they were. The coach stopped outside the Eight Bells soon after eight-twenty. The horses were watered, and, by eight-forty, the coachman cracked his whip to signal the beginning of an arduous two-hour journey back to London and the tracking of an arsonist. The only clue Crawford had to go on was the mention of Lloyd's, which he assumed meant Lloyd's of London. During the two-hour journey, Crawford gave a brief history of Lloyd's to his companions by telling them that the Company has a colourful history, springing up from a small coffee shop in Tower Street under the management of Edward Lloyd in 1688. As Lloyd's status as brokers steadily grew, its underwriting it evolved into a successful formal society that became second to none. The business moved closer to the centre of London in 1774 when the subscribers of the company moved to the Royal Exchange at Cornhill.

'When we get back to London, I will have to brief the Prime Minister on what we as an agency have uncovered. What we don't know yet is when Aston intends to set his fire. He may decide to celebrate New Year's Eve with a gigantic firework display', and Crawford wasn't underestimating the dangers.

New Year's Eve came and went, and by the beginning of the second week of January, the Prime Minister was worried if Crawford's team had been misled. Melbourne and his home secretary, Lord John Russell, along with other senior members of the administration, were questioning the reliability of Crawford's intelligence, as they couldn't understand why a man could betray a member of his own family. 'Not that a politician would ever do such a thing', Hill piped in.

By Monday, the eighth day of January, Crawford was also feeling uneasy by the way Kefford had so quickly betrayed his brother-in-law. Perhaps he was too eager to pin-point a location. Kefford, if he had he made a mockery out of Crawford's team, was either incredibly honest or damn stupid. The Royal Exchange at Cornhill had been under close surveillance for nearly a month, and all remained quiet. At mid-day on Tuesday, the ninth of January, there had been a false alarm when an old man and his dog lingered too long on the steps that led to the main doors of the Royal Exchange. But the old chap turned out to be nothing more than an innocent passer-by. At least it kept everyone on their toes, especially when twenty Peelers surrounded the old man. Hill, ever the joker, told Lizzie his money was still on the dog.

Viscount Melbourne was concerned about the escalating costs involved in keeping the Royal Exchange under twenty-four-hour watch and decided to reduce the number of officers on duty from twenty to just five during the hours of darkness and from twenty to ten during the rest of the day. Crawford tried all lenient means to change the Prime Minister's mind. Hill even overheard Crawford calling the Prime Minister 'a bloody stubborn bastard,' which he undoubtedly was.

On Tuesday, the tenth day of January, Crawford was awakened from his bed by fists hammering on the front door of his rented house at Westminster. He checked his pocket watch for the time; it was only ten minutes past midnight. His wife had as usual prepared a clean white shirt, cravat, black suit, underclothes, shoes and socks, and his favourite top hat for any eventuality, as was her wanted custom whenever her husband was on duty, in case he was required during the early hours. By the time he arrived at the scene of the fire, it was forty minutes past midnight and the flames had already reached the east side of the Exchange. It was a very cold and frosty night when the nearby watchman from the Bank of England raised the alarm for what proved to be one of London's most spectacular fires of the nineteenth century. Hill was already in attendance, along with Vickers and Lizzie, together with over fifty Peelers and countless firemen. Crawford wondered if Aston was among the onlookers, satisfied with his work and taking pride in his vocation. Crawford involuntary found himself gazing into the faces of the curious onlookers, but he didn't see Aston within the crowd of on-lookers, and that bothered him. Normally arsonists loved to witness their work.

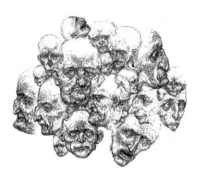

'Gazing into the faces of the curious onlookers'

CHAPTER 15

Royal Exchange

By the time the fire crew got to work, the fire had secured a firm hold in the north-west corner of the Exchange, occupied by Lloyd's Coffee House, and the flames were spreading quickly to the west side of the building, steadily consuming a row of offices belonging to the Royal Exchange Assurance. Cornhill was a residential area at this time, and the fire soon attracted large crowds who flocked into the streets, in spite of the intense cold. The Lord Mayor, accompanied by the military, arrived on the scene soon after Crawford's team. The nearby bridges crossing the Thames were crowded with people, and the flames were clearly visible twenty-four miles away at Windsor Castle.

Within half an hour, the north and west sides of the quadrangle were covered in flames and the fire had rapidly approached the clock tower. Crawford was concerned of the tower collapsing; it would undoubtedly destroy the row of houses opposite, causing immeasurable mayhem amid the increasing number of onlookers standing in the streets below.

The Lord Mayor ordered the military to evacuate the local inhabitants from their homes and move back to the safety of St. Michael's Church. The clock tower bells began chiming irregularly for a full ten minutes until the fire reached the bell tower where the bells' mechanism was rapidly being consumed by flames. Eventually, one after another, the bells fell to the floor with one almighty crash, carrying everything within its path that barred their descent to the pavement. The interior of the clock tower was filled with fire, and the crowd's attention was caught by the huge face of the clock that was glowing red hot as if from a scene from Dante's inferno. The statues around the walls within the Great Hall crashed to the ground and fractured into hundreds of shards, until miraculously, the only two statues left untouched were those of King Charles and Sir Thomas Gresham, the man who built the first Exchange during the reign of Elizabeth.

By half past three in the morning, the flames had reached the east side of the Exchange, threatening the destruction of the shops and houses in Sweeting's Alley. The people on both sides of the alley succeeded in removing most of their furniture and goods, to allow the firemen to get up onto the roofs of the houses on the side of the alley farthest from the fire enabling them to direct their hoses onto the shops and houses below. But it was impossible to save the eastern wing of the Exchange. The flames had spread from floor to floor, and within a few hours, the entire building had been reduced to ash. The blaze raged virtually unchecked throughout the night and into the early hours of Thursday morning.

When daylight eventually came, the streets were crowded with thousands of onlookers, and towards midday, one of the fire crew members succeeded in entering the building to salvage a safe thought to contain bank notes, cheques, and valuable ledgers, although the vast majority of the cash had been destroyed. By Thursday afternoon, the fire had been nearly brought under control and, according to James Braidwood's report, the buildings that had been destroyed were the Royal Exchange, the Royal Exchange Assurance office, the Gresham Committee rooms, Lloyd's rooms and the Lord Mayor's offices. Braidwood continued his report by informing the press that an inquiry would be held into the cause of the fire; however, in his view, the likely cause was an overheated stove in Lloyd's rooms.

In spite of the difficulties the firemen had to deal with, notably the extreme cold that froze their equipment and the fact that the fire had been raging for the best part of three hours before they could tackle it, the fire-fighting system was severely criticised. It was alleged that there were neither sufficient firemen nor fire engines in number to combat the fire, with some of the engines at their disposal often idle for want of trained men, with the periodical John Bull particularly scathing in its criticism by reporting that had the engines been in good, working order and capable of propelling great bodies of water, as the old fire engines used to, a greater part of the Exchange could have been saved.

Some of the engines at the west and south ends of the building could not thrust the water any higher than the first-floor windows, and even then they were incapable of breaking the glass using mere force of the water alone. Ice and stones had to be used for that purpose.

Once the fire crew deemed the area safe Crawford and his team were able to wander the perimeter of the building, Hill was livid and asked Crawford, 'Why the hell did Melbourne cut our surveillance teams?' 'Money, of course', Crawford replied. 'You will be pleased to know our country is no longer run by the politicians; you have bloody accountants to thank for this mess'. 'Well, I hope someone has deep pockets because this is going to cost a lot more than withdrawing overtime payments for fifteen Bobbies'. 'I hope no one was killed inside that furnace', Hill replied. As usual, he had to have the last word. Crawford knew his friend was right; Melbourne had been penny-pinching with calamitous results.

James Braidwood walked slowly towards a downhearted Crawford; 'Bad business this Crawford. I have just been told that besides your watchers, there was no night-watchman on duty. We now have to clean this shit up; however, I have been informed the vaults below the Exchange have unsurprisingly been covered in tons of dislodged brickwork. They seem to be more worried about their vault and its contents than checking on casualties. I fear with so much water damage I might not know about fatalities until I get the lads to clear out at least four feet of slurry from within the foundations'.

Crawford looked concerned, 'Are there any casualties?' 'Too early to say at this stage; ask me tomorrow and I might have a detailed tally. All I can confirm at the moment is that we have one man with two badly broken legs as a result of falling masonry'. Crawford wondered if the injured man was Thomas

Aston, but Braidwood confirmed the injured man was a young lad in his late teens.

Lizzie and Vickers were in a sour mood as they witnessed soldiers from the Tower trying to keep Cornhill clear.

Lizzie knew that the spread of fire could have been much worse, explaining to Sam, 'If the wind had been from the south, the Bank and St. Bartholomew's Church would have perished; we could have had another 1666 to contend with'.

Realising noting could be achieved by remaining at the Royal Exchange, Crawford suggested his team should retire to the comfort of their Whitehall office. 'We're just in their way here; best leave it to Braidwood and his men. No doubt they will determine the cause of the fire and the reason why it spread so quickly'.

Lord Hill surveyed the scene of devastation that lay before him before offering judgement. 'I'm not sure if we could have prevented this, but our task would have been easier if the rug hadn't been pulled from beneath our feet'.

Crawford could only agree with his friend. 'I've had enough of this, David. How can we do our jobs when we have one hand tied behind our back?'

'Are you sure we only have one hand tied behind our back? At times, I think it's both', Lizzie argued. 'What are our so-called leaders doing? They say they want us to protect them, but all they worry about is how much it's going to cost'. Crawford ordered his team back to Whitehall. 'Let's get back to the office. I've had enough of this'. The walk took them just under an hour, giving Crawford time to think. By the time they returned, he felt tired and dejected. He sank into his office chair. He had only been in his post for four years, and in that time he had worked under four Prime Ministers. He felt the weight of financial restrictions dragging him down. He was beginning to think that Hill was right about politicians and their continued meddling in things they clearly didn't understand.

He glanced at Lord Hill. 'Maybe it's time to call it a day. They need a younger person in charge'. 'If you're too old, what about me?' Hill joked.

Hill had seldom seen his friend looking as bleak as he was now. 'What are your intentions?' he asked. 'Close the file on the case and call it a day. I have lost faith in our leaders'.

'Bloody hell!' Hill shouted. 'Took your time coming to that conclusion'.

'I mean every word', Crawford revealed, 'I've had enough of broken promises. I honestly think some of our leaders make promises simply for the pleasure of breaking them'.

Hill sympathised with his friend. 'It ain't just the English who lie and break promises. Every leader in every land breaks their word when it suits their cause. I remember Bonaparte being transferred from the Bellerophon to the Northumberland at anchored

189

off Tor Bay. I asked him if he had any intentions to return to France. He understood my question, and I was surprised by his answer. He smiled as he tapped his nose thrice with his right index finger before looking me in the eye to give his reply. He told me the best way to keep one's word is not to give it'.

He thought about Napoleon's response before slapping Hill gently on his back. 'I can imagine Bonaparte telling you that, but I fear you're telling me lies'. Hill returned Crawford's smile and laughed. 'How can you tell?'

Crawford's general appearance was one of abject misery; he looked disconsolate and melancholic. Hill might be a pain in the arse, but he was a good pain in the arse to have about you.

'I have a meeting with Braidwood this afternoon. We need to search through the rubble of the Royal Exchange. Please say you will join me. I'm in need of company'.

'What about Sam Vickers and Lizzie Drew?' Hill enquired. 'Yes, good idea, if both of us intend to hang up our inquisitive minds, we will have to make sure our successors accrue as much knowledge as they are able to amass'.

'Best be careful, I've been told too much knowledge can be a dangerous thing'.

By the time Crawford's team arrived on site, Braidwood's men had completed their initial investigation into the cause of the fire. Due to the near total disintegration of the masonry and the supporting timbers, nothing suspicious had been found. Braidwood was perturbed as to why the flames had spread so rapidly. 'This will be my report, Mister Crawford. However, I'm unsure if it will assist you in any way as I cannot recommend or reject the report's findings. There are too many abnormalities'.

Braidwood continued giving his verbal report confirming just one person injured, and, by good fortune, no fatalities. 'We must be thankful for small mercies'. Crawford was anxious to know if it was possible for anyone to have broken into the building. Braidwood knew Crawford had an arsonist at the back of his mind, but he could neither confirm nor deny this theory. 'There is insufficient evidence to point one way or the other. The only curious occurrence appears to be an old mongrel tethered to the railings at one of the rear exits. My men are caring for the animal as we speak. I don't know if this has any bearing on the subject'. Crawford instinctively knew Aston had been responsible, but why did he abandon his dog?

'Why abandon the dog?'

CHAPTER 16

Submission and domination

Crawford requested Hill and Lizzie to accompany him back to Hatfield and the Eight Bells, his principle reason for returning being the return of one dog to its rightful owner. He also needed to know if Aston was alive or dead – not that he expected the Keffords to volunteer any information. The coach arrived outside the tavern just before midday, an unfortunate arrival time as the rain was falling in torrents. The coach driver pulled the horses up immediately outside the hostelry in a futile attempt to keep his passengers from a good soaking. Crawford appreciated the gesture and palmed a half-crown to the driver before swiftly disappearing inside the Eight Bells. Crawford glanced about the interior of the tavern, which was empty save for Silas and Julia Kefford leaning against the bar, both of whom wore glum expressions. Crawford was unaware if their guise was for his benefit or if trade of late had declined to such an extent that they were wasting their time opening the doors.

The Keffords sneered indifferently at Crawford's arrival as they menacingly moved to the front of the bar. If Silas Kefford fancied a verbal slanging match or worse, Crawford was satisfied he had his enforcer with him. He considered defusing the probability of an uninvited quarrel by altering his approach – perhaps a welcoming handshake would placate Kefford's aggression. Alas, Crawford's outstretched hand was slapped aside! Lord Hill stepped menacingly forward, but Crawford, diplomatic till the end, a firm believer that the pen was always mightier than the sword despite the provocation being thrown back in his face, remained firm in his principles by insisting neither threats nor harassment could ever win a fight over him.

Noticing the menacing grimace on Hill's face, Silas began to back-off, but his wife remained unforgiving and intolerant to Crawford and his team, threatening retribution against her own husband unless Silas delivered her vengeance.

Lizzie thought she might stand a better chance of mediation and stepped forward to face Silas Kefford, who was quivering, unable to comprehend what his objective should be. 'We have simply come to return your uncle's dog'. Silas looked at the dog as it trembled in fear by Lizzie's side. Common sense prevailed within Silas brain, but Julia's eye's remained glazed, perhaps anticipating that Lizzie's controlling, hypnotic mind still had powers over her browbeaten husband. 'Will you please sit down, Silas?' Crawford pointed to a convenient chair near the bar. 'I've no quarrel with either of you. You must be aware of the recent arson attack at the Royal Exchange, and I am happy to inform you that luckily no one was killed. However, one young lad had his legs crushed by falling masonry. We're uncertain if he will ever walk again, let alone work'.

'You must appreciate that murder is a crime deserving of the death sentence; so far we have four deaths coupled with Thomas Aston. If either of you continue to protect a suspected criminal, you could both be sentenced as participants in his crimes. If you love your daughter – as I suspect you do – you must help us find him'. Lizzie's words resonated inside Silas's head, but Julia remained defiant. Julia spat out her words with acidy venom. 'Why should I believe you when Thomas testifies he's innocent of the crime you level against him'.

'Just consider the evidence against him', Crawford pleaded. 'If he is innocent, I will help him, but you must admit his pleas of being above suspicion reminds me of the parable concerning a house built on sand – just too hard to contemplate'.

Julia wouldn't budge from her faith in her uncle. She knew him to be incapable of such a hideous crime. Tears flowed uncontrollably down her pale checks. 'I am of his blood, I cannot envisage Thomas as anything more than a good, honest, gentle soul, maybe a shade simple'. 'I'm afraid, Misses Kefford, your assessment of Thomas Aston wouldn't sway me or a jury', Hill gravely told her. 'If you honestly think him to be blameless of these crimes, his only hope is for Mister Crawford to help him prove his innocence, and for that to happen, he has to talk to him and listen to his account – that is the only way'.

Julia held Silas tightly by the hand, still unconvinced about what she should do. 'Let me talk privately to Silas. I promise you an answer within the hour, and rest assured, we will not assist Thomas in taking flight – he's frightened and needs calming before you question him'.

The Keffords agreed to meet Crawford and his small team back at the Eight Bells at three o'clock in the afternoon. They stubbornly refused to disclose the meeting place and insisted that Lord Hill remain with Silas until Crawford, Lizzie and Julia had departed – 'deal'. 'Deal', repeated Lizzie. The three of them walked in the direction of Hatfield House before turning sharply left and ascending the slight incline that led to the church. The church door was ajar, signifying someone was waiting for them. As they gently opened the door, to Crawford's surprise it was the Reverend Boothby who welcomed the small group into the church and ushered them towards the altar, where a lone defected figure sat, arms folded, staring at a faded painting of Christ's crucifixion.

Thomas Aston appeared out of place in the House of God, looking dismal and dishevelled. Crawford felt pity towards the man, but if proved guilty of the crimes of arson and murder, pity would soon evaporate and the full force of justice would shatter upon his head.

Lizzie touched Crawford's sleeve and gently asked if she could talk to Aston first. With a slight nod of the head, Crawford agreed and sat in the pews reserved for the choir. Julia and Boothby sat on either side of Crawford, remaining quiet as they tried hard to concentrate on the impending conversation.

'We have returned the dog. Silas is caring for him. He's looking forward to being with you again'. That brought the desired affect from Aston, whose foul face suddenly brightened to reveal an immense

195

ray of sunshine and beaming smile across his grimy face.

'Thank you, kind lady', was all Aston could say, and, to be honest, those were the first words either Lizzie or Crawford had heard from the man in their long stay at Hatfield. Thomas Aston had always kept himself to himself. He enjoyed his own company and never entertained the company of others, even the company of his niece, Julia. Lizzie glanced up at Crawford in surprise. It was painfully clear that Thomas Aston was a man of few words, lacking in confidence and self-belief. Aston was still smiling as he sat cross-legged, slowly rocking his body forward and back. Lizzie stood up and walked towards Julia to enquire how long her uncle had been in this state. 'Ever since Sombreffe', she replied. 'Before that he was the joker in the pack, the life and soul of the party, but after Sombreffe, he changed, not only physically but mentally too. His friends at the old comrades' establishment acquired employment for him; he even worked inside the Prime Minister's residence for a week or so before being moved on as an embarrassment. Hestia had even gone to London to help him find lodgings. Mentally, he hasn't moved on. He thinks he is still in Sombreffe. He doesn't think of Hatfield as his home. Lizzie looked at Julia, wondering if she was the woman responsible for Aston's actions. Had she dominated her uncle into submission to carry-out these dreadful crimes, or was it the meek and mild Silas who played with Aston's mind? She couldn't tell all she knew was Thomas Aston was innocent of striking a match, let alone start a fire. Lizzie recalled the afternoon of the fire. Both Silas and Julia remained in full view; they couldn't have started the fire and Hestia had been working upstairs. They had heard her. Lizzie minded and came to an abrupt halt; she repeated those final four words to herself: 'They had heard her'. But seeing wasn't believing – it was true no one had witnessed Hestia changing the bedclothes and moving heavy furniture about; it could have been anyone. Lizzie asked Boothby if he minded asking the tavern's potman to join them. She hoped this could be swiftly cleared up.

The Reverend Boothby returned in less than six minutes with the potman in tow. She asked him if he had helped Hestia with her chores on the afternoon of the fire at the big house. He glanced at Julia before answering, 'I only helped for fifteen minutes when your daughter left to see her beau'. Julia felt betrayed. Her own daughter had somehow persuaded Aston to take her revenge against the Reverend Boyd, Parliament and the Royal Exchange, but why kill Briggs? She accepted that the Dowager Marchioness was killed by accident, but Briggs was no accident. There was another, as yet unanswered, question: Who killed Captain Edward Boyd? At the realisation of the Captain's name, Aston raised his hand. 'It was me', he said, more in apology than a confessional – 'He killed your parents and raped you' He countered. Whether this was correct Lizzie couldn't ascertain; it sounded too rehearsed for Aston's mind, unless he had been brainwashed into thinking he had been responsible.

Crawford rose from his seat and took Julia's hand. 'Where is Hestia now?', he calmly enquired. 'Right here', a voice echoed from the rear pews of the church. Julia cried out in anguish,

'Hestia, what have you done?' But Hestia, without remorse, told her mother. 'They deserved to die. I remember the nights you cried yourself to sleep when you recalled that dreadful night. You told me Silas was not my father, and I was likely the result of a rape perpetrated by Captain Boyd, the vicar's son. I did it for you, mother. You told me I was named after a Greek Goddess, but you failed to tell me I was named after a sacrificial flame. Well, I made sure I had my sacrifices. Hestia slowly stood up, holding the flaming candles in both hands. 'I'm sorry I involved Uncle Tom in my vengeance, but neither you, mother, nor your spineless husband ever considered retribution for my being. You only spat out meaningless words – action speaks louder than words, and my words will take flight from within these flames. Fire cannot hurt me, I am the deliverer of fire'. Hestia softly began to sing – 'All you have is your fire and the place you need to reach, don't ever tame your demons, but keep'em on a leash'. She stood motionless and silent as she held the candles to her clothing. The thin veil of transparency between reason and lunacy appeared to cloud within Hestia's mind; for a second, she hesitated, but it was too late to change course, as the fire burst to life, and before Crawford could rush to help, Hestia was engulfed in flames. Julia and Lizzie screamed; neither had expected Hestia's self-sacrifice. The Reverend Boothby held Aston close to his chest, desperately trying to obscure the hideous sight playing out before them. Hestia in death was laughing – she achieved her goals and Aston just happened to be collateral damage.

Lizzie explained things to Crawford and the team from the start, that in her opinion two individuals had written the coded messages. She also considered one was highly intelligent and dominated the other. Aston was certainly submissive; this was confirmed when he tried to explain the murder of Briggs. Hestia had told him to put the agent out of his misery, like a little bird. In that way, Aston had understood her instructions. The killing was conducted out of mercy and for no other reason. Hestia had given him various letters and told him where to leave them; he even admitted being in an office at Whitehall, as well as leaving boxes inside the parliament buildings, the Salisbury residence and the Royal Exchange but had no idea what was in the boxes. And Aston couldn't understand why Hestia had taken his cherished dog.

Crawford failed to comprehend Hestia's suicide – the image of her blazing silhouette would live long in his memory. Did she really think that fire would embrace her and enhance her body? Did she for one second consider that the fire would bring about her end? He knew Hestia had manipulated her uncle to perform acts of terrorism that under normal circumstances he would never contemplate. Hestia was most certainly the dominant force, and Aston was nothing more than a child being guided along like a submissive partner obeying, without question, her instructions. Lizzie felt nothing but nausea and pain as she tried to console the Keffords, but nothing could explain their daughter's state of mind. Although she had been born of lust, she had been cherished in life, and at the end of her short life, her parents were left confused and bewildered. Their daughter's secret life had been well concealed. It made John Crawford think of his own family, his wife, his children and his grandchildren, some of them of a similar age to Hestia. It was time for him to stand down – he had seen terrible things in his seventy years. He had witnessed untold deaths on battlefield; he had seen the atrocities carried out by retreating armies, but the nightmare of witnessing a young woman committing suicide by fire would stay in his mind forever.

John Crawford could still smell burning flesh; his eyes were etched with visions of horror. He had had enough, time to stand down. His mind was made up; he had to retire for the sake of his own sanity and leave the agency in the hands of a younger individual. He would remain at the helm until the Queen's coronation – but no longer.

EPILOGUE

John Crawford arranged to meet the Prime Minister on the morning of Monday the second of July 1838. Queen Victoria's coronation had gone off without a hitch, despite a few dozen letters perpetrating to having been sent from would-be assassins. Lord Hill remained outside number ten. Waiting patiently within the hackney, he considered one last broadside aimed at politics in general but decided better of it – it would achieve little except to make his newly evaluated pension vanish as quickly as it appeared.

Viscount Melbourne spoke first. 'I'm most pleased that we can close the file on this dreadful arson thing'. As if the arson attacks were of little concern. Crawford was only in attendance to offer his resignation. 'I have aged considerably since my appointment to lead the agency five years ago. It's time I spent time with my wife and grandchildren; they must take priority now. Without them, I'm nothing'

Melbourne was taken aback, probably anxious to know the name of the individual Crawford deemed his successor – surely he wouldn't recommend that awful Lord Hill!

The Prime Minister once again thanked Crawford for his loyal service to Parliament and the Crown and suggested they participate in a glass of sherry. 'I assume you have someone in mind to take over your responsibilities', he enquired. 'Yes, Prime Minister', Crawford quickly responded.

It was Melbourne's turn to look impatient as he raised the glass to toast Crawford's health. The glassed clinked as Crawford named his successor, 'Lizzie Drew'. That got Melbourne's attention.

'A woman? Are you out of your mind, Crawford?' Melbourne was flustered; he tried to grasp the words of objection but none came, as the sherry dribbled from his lips. 'Just think, Prime Minister', Crawford attempted to explain his reasoning. 'She's bright, young, clever, energetic and ambitious; all the qualifications needed to head the agency'. 'But she's a woman'. It was all Melbourne could offer in the way of a meaningful objection.

Crawford thought about saying 'So is your wife' but decided to try a different tact. 'So is the Queen, and you will be dancing around her to win her favours'. Melbourne looked shocked. How could Crawford suggest Lizzie Drew as his successor and compare her with his relationship with the Queen of England? 'Just think, Prime Minister, no one would ever realise the head of England's secret service was a woman; she would be invisible in plain sight, if you get my meaning'.

'But she's a woman', Melbourne repeated. 'You cannot consider a woman; they don't count. They should be at home bringing up children and doing needlework'. 'I wouldn't like your wife hear you say that', Crawford advised him. 'One day, women will have the vote. They might possibly rise to the status of a cabinet rank, to become Prime Minister might be asking too much, but anything is possible'. Again, Melbourne's sole response was, 'But she's a woman'.

'You've asked me for my recommendation; if you want to accept my advice that is fair enough. If you don't, be it on your own head. In my humble opinion, Lizzie Drew, the daughter of a Lord of the realm, would be most admirable for the post. I must take my leave, as Lord Hill and I have an appointment on the golf course'.

Melbourne looked extremely unhappy as he kept muttering to himself, 'She's a woman'.

HISTORICAL NOTES AND EXPLANATIONS

George Maynard married Sarah Harle at St. John the Evangelist Church, Lambeth on the sixth day of October 1833. The rest of the novel, except where historical facts can confirm to the contrary.

John Bellingham did assassinate Spencer Percival within the lobby of the House of Commons. His motive for killing the Prime Minister of England is as described in this novel. John Bellingham paid the ultimate price for his deeds and was hung at Newgate Prison, London three days after his trial.

England's secret intelligence agency did exist, but not until 1909. During the early days of the service, they had a staff of sixteen, including one caretaker. I have taken the liberty of starting the bureau seventy-five years earlier.

Cold reading is a set of techniques used by mentalists, psychics, fortune-tellers, mediums, illusionists and scam artists to imply that they know more about a person than they actually do. A psychic purports to be a person who claims to use extrasensory perception (ESP) to identify information hidden from the normal senses, involving telepathy or clairvoyance.

The Cato Street conspiracy is a fact and five of the accused were hung, drawn and quartered. George Edwards was a police spy under the control of John Stafford, but for the benefit of the story line is sounded better to have his controller as John Crawford.

Chinese whispers refers to a sequence of repetitions of a story, each one differing slightly from the original, so that the final telling bears only a scant resemblance to the original.

Thomas Skelton was a court jester of sorts to Moncuster Castle in Britain in the 16th century. He was the last jester or fool to the Pennington's; he was known as Tom Fool and was responsible for the phrase 'tomfoolery'.

The expression 'spilling the beans' means to divulge a secret, especially to do so inadvertently or maliciously.

The well-known nursery rhythm 'oranges and lemons' have various versions and meanings. I respectfully suggest that the last line is very important as it points out the location of Bow bells, where traditionally cockneys vehemently claim. To be a cockney you must be born within the sound of Bow bells. Bromley-by-Bow in East London is certainly not the location of the great bell at Bow. To discover the great bell at Bow, you have to look towards Eastcheap – namely St. Mary-le-Bow. There are various reasons why Bromley-by-Bow church appeals to the cockney clan as being the rightful place of their originalities. Many churches across the world have had their bells cast by the Whitechapel Bell Foundry, but arguably its best-known examples are not in places of worship. In 1752, the foundry cast the Liberty Bell, which was commissioned to celebrate the 50th anniversary of William Penn's 1701 Charter of Privileges Pennsylvania's original constitution. As a result of damage sustained during its stormy passage across the Atlantic, the bell cracked when it was first rung, and after repeated repairs, cracked again in 1846 when rung to mark the birthday of George Washington. Since 2003, the bell has been housed at the Liberty Bell Centre near Independence Hall. Big Ben, which tolls the hour at the Palace of Westminster, was cast in 1858 and rung for the first time on 31st May 1859. Big Ben weighs 13½ tons and is the largest bell ever cast at the foundry. Big Ben also cracked because the hammer that was initially used was too heavy. The crack and the subsequent retuning gave Big Ben its present distinctive tone. A profile template of Big Ben surrounds the entrance door of the Whitechapel Foundry, while the original moulding gauge is retained near the furnaces. The final bill for Big Ben cost £572.

A final word on the Whitechapel foundry: it was here that the bells for Saint Mary-Le-Bow Church, Cheapside were cast.

The chapter referring to John Flamsteed, Isaac Newton and Edmund Halley is accurate. If anyone is interested in checking the facts, I suggest you check out any computers search engine.

In 1834, the Exchequer was faced with the problem of disposing two cart-loads of wooden tally sticks. These were remnants of an obsolete accounting system that had not been used since 1826. When asked to burn them, the Clerk of Works thought that the two underfloor stoves in the basement of the House of Lords would be a safe and proper place to do so. On 16 October, a couple of workmen arrived in the morning to carry out his instructions. During the afternoon, a party of visitors to the House of Lords, conducted by the deputy housekeeper Mrs. Wright, became puzzled by the heat of the floor, and by the smoke seeping through it. But the workmen insisted on finishing their job. The furnaces were put out by five o'clock and Mrs. Wright, no longer worried, locked up the premises. At six o'clock, Mrs. Wright heard the terrified wife of a doorkeeper screaming that the House of Lords was on fire. In no time, the flames had spread to the rest of the palace. The fire was a great sight for the crowds on the streets, who were kept back by soldiers, and a great opportunity for artists such as J.M.W. Turner who painted several canvases depicting it. Both Houses of Parliament were destroyed along with most of the other buildings on the site. Westminster Hall was saved largely due to heroic fire-fighting efforts, and a change in the direction of the wind during the night. The only other parts of the Palace to survive were the Jewel Tower, the Undercroft Chapel, the Cloisters and Chapter House of Saint Stephen's and Westminster Hall.

'The Spider and the Fly' is the title of a poem written by Mary Howitt. The poem was published in 1828 and is a cautionary tale against those who use flattery and charm to disguise their true evil intentions, very much like the language used by politicians.

William IV was called 'The Sailor King' due to the fact that he joined the navy at the tender age of fourteen. He served around the coasts of the United States and the West Indies. He was promoted to admiral in 1811 at the age of forty-six. Not bad for the crusty British Navy. William then rose to be Lord High Admiral in 1827. Another of William's nicknames was 'Silly Billy'. Unfortunately, this term was used to describe a particular London clown and became a very common name for fairground clowns during the nineteenth century.

Queen Victoria's accession to the throne marked the dawn of a new era in Britain's history, representing industrial growth, scientific advances and vast imperial expansion. The British public, it seemed, wholly supported their new Queen. This good humour would fluctuate greatly over the following six decades, but it was a promising start to her reign. The sun had risen on the Victorian era, and it would not set until the early twentieth century.

Queen Victoria 1837-1901
Queen of Great Britain and Ireland, Empress of India

Hatfield House was partially destroyed by fire late in November 1835. The fire took the life of the Mary Amelia, better known as 'Emily Cecil' the First Marchioness of Salisbury, who was a prominent Tory party hostess. I have taken the liberty of delaying the fire by two full years, thereby adding to the problems that accrued in 1837. The account of the fire as mentioned in chapter four is most accurate.

The expression 'to shut the stable door after the horse has bolted,' dates from medieval times. In chapter four, Lord Hill attempts to reverse the old saying by telling John Crawford that he has left the door to the chicken run wide open for an intruder (or in this case the fox) before closing the gate.

The expression, 'when the shit hits the fan' – or as Crawford mentions, 'hits the door' – dates back to only pre-Second World War. John Crawford, being a wily old fox, is just the sort of man who could turn much later expressions into his own around one hundred years earlier.

The modern meaning of screwed, or to screw-up, originated from the middle of the sixteenth century with a meaning to screw as 'exerting pressure or coercion', probably in reference to instruments of torture (e.g. thumbscrews). It quickly gained a wider general sense of 'in a bind; in unfortunate inescapable circumstances'. When the verb 'to screw' gained a sexual connotation in the early seventeenth century, it joined a long-lasting association with sexual imagery. I leave the rest for the reader to contemplate.

The game of hawk-dove, later to be known as chicken or the snowdrift game, is a model of conflict between two players in game theory. The principle of the game is that while it is to both players' benefit if one player yields, the other player's optimal choice depends on what his opponent is doing: if his opponent yields, the player should not, but if the opponent fails to yield, the player should; or as Crawford explained the rules – who blinks first.

The expression 'nightcap' simply means an alcoholic drink taken at bedtime or at the end of a festive evening.

A white lie is a harmless or trivial lie, especially if told to avoid hurting someone's feelings.

A mantrap was a mechanical physical security device for catching poachers or trespassers. They have taken many forms, the most usual being like a large foothold trap, the steel springs being armed with teeth which met in the victim's leg. Since 1827, they have been illegal in England, except in houses between sunset and sunrise as a defence against burglars.

The expression 'to get one's two pennies in' means a discussion on which you have a right to an opinion; if you have your two penn'orth or put in your two penn'orth, you are simply adding your opinion to the discussion.

The expression regarding 'ifs and buts' originates from a long-forgotten sixteenth century poem.

If wishes were horses then beggars would ride,
if turnips were swords I'd have one by my side.
If ifs and buts were pots and pans
there'd be no work for tinkers' hands!

The expression 'hair standing up on the back of one's neck' has its origins in an old saying: when you experience a peculiar feeling and are not able to put your finger on why you feel so, but your body instantly tells you that something is not right.

Goosebumps are a physiological phenomenon inherited from our animal ancestors, which was useful to them but are not of much help to us. Goosebumps are tiny elevations of the skin that resemble the skin of poultry after the feathers have been plucked. The reason for all these responses is the subconscious release of a stress hormone called adrenaline. In humans, adrenaline is produced in two small beanlike glands that sit atop the kidneys; it not only causes the contraction of the skin muscles but also influences many other body reactions.

General John Millett Hamerton did exist and served gallantly at Quatra-Bras; Captain Edward Boyd is a factious character.

A potman is a person who is employed within a public house to collect empty pots and glasses.

As previous mentioned, the fire at Hatfield House took place in November 1835, and not in November 1837; however, the brief description of the fire as reported in chapter 7 is very close to the truth. The Dowager's jewellery was lost, although robbery was never considered a motive for the blaze. The disappearance of her jewels was solely considered the effects of the fire at Hatfield House.

A provost marshal was part of a department that was in charge of discipline in Wellington's army; a little like the military police, they saw that crimes were tried and punished, oversaw executions, and so on.

Saint Etheldreda's Church was the town chapel of the Bishops of Ely from about 1250 to 1570. It is the oldest Catholic Church in England and one of only two remaining buildings in London from the reign of Edward I. It was once one of the most influential places in London with a palace of vast grounds. It was like an independent state, the Bishop of Ely's place in London or Ely Place as it is now called, and its chapel took its name from one of England's most popular saints of the day, Etheldreda. Princess Etheldreda, daughter of King Anna, a prominent member of the ruling family of the Kingdom of East Anglia, was born in 630. She wanted to be a nun but agreed to a political marriage with a neighbouring King, Egfrith, on condition that she could remain a virgin. When the King tried to break the agreement, she fled back to Ely, where, as well as founding a religious community, she also built a magnificent church on the ruins of one founded by the efforts of St Augustine himself but laid waste by war. Etheldreda was quite a revolutionary. She set free all the bondsmen on her lands and, for seven years, led a life of exemplary austerity. After her death in 679, devotion towards her spread rapidly as people received help and favours through what they were convinced was her powerful intercession in Heaven. And when, through popular demand, it was decided to remove her to a more fitting tomb, it was found that even after 15 years in wet earth her body was still in a perfect state of preservation. When the Normans began building the present Cathedral at Ely and moved her body in 1106, it was again reported to be still uncorrupted. That was nearly 450 years after her death. Hatfield village, as it stood in the reign of Queen Victoria, is accurately portrayed within the book, with the exception of the name of the vicar. When this book was first written, the incumbent at Saint Etheldreda Church was the Reverend Julie Boothby, so this is the name I opted for this novel. However, as females were not ordained until 1994, I had little choice than to name the incumbent as simply 'Boothby'.

With reference to William Edward Boyd and his son Edward, these are all fictitious characters.

St. Etheldreda Church, Hatfield

The meaning of the expression to go 'doolally', simply meant to go mad, originating from the Indian garrison town of Deolali, where British soldiers waited, sometimes for months, to be taken back to Britain after their tour of duty. There was nothing to do and many may have been suffering from Post-Traumatic Stress Disorder, initiating madness.

In the eighteenth century, 'mumbo jumbo' referred to a West African God. The Concise Oxford English Dictionary states that 'Mumbo Jumbo' was the name of a grotesque idol said to have been worshipped by some tribes. In its figurative sense, Mumbo Jumbo is an object of senseless veneration or a meaningless ritual.

If a person jumped out of their skin, they experience a physical symptom of withdrawal or flinching especially when connected to fear or surprise.

Hestia was the virgin goddess of the hearth (both private and municipal) and the home. As the goddess of the family hearth, she also presided over the cooking of bread and the preparation of the family meal. Hestia was also the goddess of the sacrificial flame and received a share of every sacrifice to the Gods.

When you say that something will happen 'as sure as eggs are eggs', it means that it will happen certainly and without a doubt.

Few of us are aware that many commonly used words or expressions once had other meanings –

in many cases, quite the opposite as those now current. In this context, the word 'right' within the phrase 'as right as rain,' originally meant straight (in terms of direction).

Biting one's tongue means a person wanting to say something that may be offensive or hurtful that is best not to say at all.

Momento Mori is the Medieval Latin Christian theory and practice of reflection on mortality, especially as a means of considering the vanity of earthly life and the transient nature of all earthly goods and pursuits. It is related to the ars moriendi ('The Art of Dying') and similar Western literature. Memento Mori has been an important part of ascetic disciplines as a means of perfecting one's character by cultivating detachment and other virtues, and by turning one's attention towards the immortality of the soul and the afterlife.

The expression 'humbug' means something designed to deceive and mislead. To put it another way – when a wilfully false, deceptive, or insincere person tells you something that is not correct, they are talking 'humbug'.

This book has numerous factual connections, but it is nevertheless a work of fiction, and that being the case, it must be noted that there was never a massacre at the Belgium village of Sombreffe.

The well-known Christmas Carol 'Silent Night' was originally written as a poem by an Austrian priest named Joseph Mohr. On Christmas

Eve in 1818 in the small alpine village of Oberndorf, the church organ was found to be in a state of disrepair. Joseph Mohr therefore gave the poem 'Stille Nacht', or 'Silent Night' in English to his friend Franz Xavier Gruber. The melody and music for 'Silent Night' was composed for the guitar and the simple score was finished in time for Midnight Mass. 'Silent Night' is the most famous Christmas carol of all time, with its beautiful lyrics conveying the essence of peace and love.

The expression 'two's company, three's a crowd' arises from an old proverb and is an informal way to express a situation where two people desire privacy and a third person is present. There is an additional variant to the above proverb that states two is company but three is none: two's a couple, but three's a crowd, four's too many, and fives's not allowed. Don't ask me to express a view on this variant!

The report and medical symptoms of cholera as described within this novel are most accurate.

First Footing is a tradition celebrated at Hogmanay, a Scottish New Year's celebration. It is supposed to bring good luck and prosperity to the household in the New Year.

The fire at the Royal Exchange in January 1838 has been well-documented; together with the scathing report criticising the fire crew and their engines, it is most accurate. There was no night-watchman supervising the building on the night of the fire, but, more importantly to the reader, this novel although based on historical fact and fiction that has been interwoven, is nonetheless fiction. There wasn't any surveillance of the building as there never was an arson threat.

The Arsonist's Lullaby, written by Hozier, featured in the television program *The Walking Dead.*

The Representation of the People Act 1918 saw British women over the age of 30 secure the vote. The Equal Franchise Act of 1928 lowered the voting age for women from 30 to 21. Margaret Thatcher, a grocer's daughter from Grantham, who had served as leader of the Conservative Party since February 1975, became Britain's first female Prime Minister with a 44-seat majority in the House of Commons. She went on to become the longest-serving prime minister of the 20th century, remaining in power until November 1990. After losing the leadership of the party to John Major, she served as a back-bencher for an additional two years. She died on 8th April 2013.

Pandora's box

Hestia, the Greek Goddess of the sacrificial flame

Printed in Great
Britain
by Amazon